RAVENSCRAG

RAVENSCRAG

A NOVEL

ALAIN FARAH

*

Translated by
Lazer Lederhendler

ARACHNIDE

This edition published in 2015 by
House of Anansi Press Inc.
110 Spadina Avenue, Suite 801
Toronto, ON, M5V 2K4
Tel. 416-363-4343
Fax 416-363-1017
www.houseofanansi.com

Distributed in Canada by
HarperCollins Canada Ltd.
1995 Markham Road
Scarborough, ON, M1B 5M8
Toll free tel. 1-800-387-0117

House of Anansi Press is committed to protecting our natural environment. As part of our efforts, the interior of this book is printed on paper that contains 100% post-consumer recycled fibres, is acid-free, and is processed chlorine-free.

19 18 17 16 15   1 2 3 4 5

Library and Archives Canada Cataloguing in Publication
Farah, Alain, 1979–,
[Pourquoi Bologne. English]
    Ravenscrag : a novel / by Alain Farah ; translated by Lazer Lederhendler.
Translation of: Pourquoi Bologne.
Issued in print and electronic formats.
ISBN 978-1-77089-895-0 (pbk.). — ISBN 978-1-77089-896-7 (html)
    I. Lederhendler, Lazer, 1950–, translator II. Title.
III. Title: Pourquoi Bologne. English

PS8611.A72P6813 2015   C843'.6   C2014-906575-2
                                                C2014-906576-0

Book design: Alysia Shewchuk

Canada Council Conseil des Arts
for the Arts   du Canada

ONTARIO ARTS COUNCIL
CONSEIL DES ARTS DE L'ONTARIO
an Ontario government agency
un organisme du gouvernement de l'Ontario

We acknowledge for their financial support of our publishing program the Canada Council for the Arts, the Ontario Arts Council, and the Government of Canada through the Canada Book Fund. We acknowledge the financial support of the Government of Canada, through the National Translation Program for Book Publishing, an initiative of the Roadmap for Canada's Official Languages 2013–2018: Education, Immigration, Communities, for our translation activities.

Printed and bound in Canada

For Yolande Safi
For the deaths we have lived through

RAVENSCRAG

IN INTERGALACTIC SPACE, where it's nice to take refuge at times, our vessel floats among the stars. I step closer to the TV and a deep voice says, "In the future, in the year 2012, war was beginning."

An explosion shakes the ship. The captain exclaims, "What happen?"

The mechanic is quick to reply. "Somebody set up us the bomb!"

I whistle a cheerful tune and slip my hand into my pocket. I grasp the pillbox that Dr. Cameron gave me, but, no, I let it go.

With my eyes glued to the TV, I reassure the captain: "We get signal. Main screen turn on."

The face of a dwarf multiplies on the console monitors. The background shifts from blue to red. The evil commodore speaks to us in a mocking tone of voice.

"How are you gentlemen? All you base are belong to us! You are on the way to destruction."

I try to warn the captain, yelling at the top of my lungs so that my words pass through the screen. I tell him not to submit to the dwarf's blackmail, that I'm on my way with reinforcements. But I'm not sure that he hears me and, in fact, a moment later he asks, "What you say?"

The commodore breaks in. Gracefully attired in his amethyst cape, which gives him the complexion of a corpse, he lifts his arms skyward as he addresses the captain, the mechanic, and me.

"You have no chance to survive. Make your time, ha, ha, ha, ha…"

This is bad. I'm in a state. I'm afraid to die. I switch off the TV.

Just then, Édouard calls me.

*

Enjoying the comfort of one's apartment, slouched in a loveseat upholstered in French terry, following a good sci-fi series on the television… who could be so zealous as to deny himself that?

Me, who else.

It's been just a few months since I was hired at McGill

University, but I'm so swamped with work that I spend all my time there, from noon to midnight.

I'm surrounded by various objects laid out on my desk: a black marble bust of Edgar Poe, a metal box where I keep a picture of the Catholic orphanage, and a toy soldier lying in the prone position with his weapon aimed at me as a reminder that some people wish to do me harm.

The thing I like most in this room dates back to another century. It's the wood-frame window, almost three metres high, directly behind me. I'm aware of my lack of caution. A man armed with a high-precision rifle, in the grip of madness or under contract to take me down, hidden behind the perforated venetian blind of his apartment, could easily shoot me in the back of the neck without my ever noticing the laser sight.

I turn around. It's snowing.

My window looks out on avenue McGregor and the McTavish reservoir. Every day at exactly twelve noon, the wind picks up on the promontory where Montreal stores its water supply. Gusts of powdered snow swirl about, and the snow drifts against the window. The elements have joined forces to present me with a private storm.

"A private storm…"

Before coming to McGill, I could never have allowed myself to utter such an expression, a short, simple, beautiful phrase charged with feeling. I was an experimental writer, a dry, phlegmatic man.

6   ALAIN FARAH

A few months ago, things changed. I changed.

Are the voices in our heads the first to warn us of a problem? Is a pastoral poet who converts to the avant-garde necessarily the victim of a plot?

*

Colleagues often wonder what I'm up to and come knocking on my office door. I try to stay calm and answer, "I'm writing."

They go away.

If you bump into me at a cocktail party, you won't notice my discomfort. My good humour will surprise you, as will my easy conversation and storytelling. You'll find me likeable, with my electronic cigarette and my designer-label ties. You may be tempted to check if there's a writer hiding under my elegant affability. Then you'll go so far as to visit a bookstore and buy one of my books. Against all odds, you'll read it.

Ordinarily, at this point, it's a given that things will go sour. You'll fret over not finding the right words to pretend that you found my book "interesting." The next time you bump into me at a cocktail party, I'll sense your embarrassment and tell you so.

But none of this matters in the slightest.

My stories—I may as well own up to it right from the outset—I tear my stories to pieces for the sole purpose of translating the telescoped experience of my time periods.

The year is 1962.

I don't know where I come from or where I'm going. Connections are a problem for me. When I look in the mirror, my eyes, my nose, my mouth are mine. But can things really be that simple? How can I be sure that my face isn't entirely different, entirely another, that if I crossed paths with myself on the street I would recognize me?

Me — this is me telling this to myself.

For the past few weeks, my health has been declining. That's why I must pay Dr. Cameron a visit. I'm going to tell you about him, a great deal about him. But let's take things one step at a time. I don't like to rush people.

★

For a long time, my cousin Édouard would come with me to the cinema when I was granted furlough at the orphanage. He was always understanding about my spells, which would happen right in the middle of the show. I would leave the theatre abruptly, overcome by fits of nausea or by visual disorientation bordering on distraction.

I was obsessed back then by the phenomenon of persistence of vision; my mind tried to outmanoeuvre it, to see not the flow of moving images, but pictures independent of one another.

My cousin would find me in the washroom, where he would cool my forehead with soaking wet brown paper towel, which soon turned lumpy.

"Is it the news about the war in Vietnam that affects you like this?"

"Édouard, I have a feeling we're headed for disaster."

I didn't want to worry him by admitting that what truly terrorized me at the movies was my inability to perceive the continuous movement of people and things on the screen, so I would always come up with a relatively silly excuse to explain my attacks.

My fragmented perception of pictures in darkened theatres is the second reason I prefer television. The first reason? Well, that will come second.

*

For the past few weeks I've been having trouble concentrating. This morning in front of the mirror, for instance, in an attempt to stop thinking about my eyes, my nose, my mouth, to hush the voices in my head saying maybe this was not my face after all, I tried to concentrate on knotting my tie in the Double Windsor without which I never leave the apartment. I told myself it would do me good to indulge in the mental description of this perfunctory gesture, repeated a thousand times; I convinced myself that with a step-by-step commentary on each of the three or four folds that guarantee my elegance, tying my tie would silence the voices in my head telling me my face is not my face. Unfortunately, that's not quite what happened. My hands fluttered wildly, and I had to start the knot over nearly ten times. I had an urge to smash my fist into the mirror, movie-style, but I was afraid of what the voices might say then. In any case, I'm not in a film, and one obsession in particular haunts me more than any other: If an intelligence agency were to penetrate my thoughts, would I be aware of it? In my head, I constantly hear this statement by Kissinger, who some see as the future head of U.S. diplomacy: "Just because you're paranoid doesn't mean they're not after you." Neat, don't you think? But, more to the point, how do you manage to go on, knowing this, feeling it?

*

Looks are deceiving—Plato already had a lot to say on the subject.

Personally, it's enough for me to think about the Mechanical Turk—the automaton reputed to be unbeatable at chess that subdued Benjamin Franklin and the first Napoleon—to be afflicted by dizziness.

People's fascination with the Turk arose from its ability to read the minds of its adversaries, to anticipate each of their moves. It was at once feared and admired. Edgar Poe, in "Maelzel's Chess Player," even referred to it as the greatest invention of all time.

One day, however, the Turk revealed its secret. Hidden behind a set of mirrors was a homunculus, a homely, hunchback, midget chess master, endowed with one practical quality: he was there.

These days, we no longer know who moves the pieces — there is no Turk or chessboard anymore.

The year is 2012 and 1962.

The year is 1962 and 2012.

It's cold.

Something's not right, but what?

Someone, somewhere, is controlling us.

*

In "Maelzel's Chess Player," written in 1836 and translated into French in 1862 by Charles Baudelaire, Edgar Poe states that nothing had ever attracted as much public attention as the Mechanical Turk. Wherever it appeared, it aroused intense curiosity.

In fact, wherever one went there were people with a genius for mechanics, possessing great insight and uncommon discernment, who declared without hesitation that the automaton was a pure machine, its movements entirely unrelated to human actions, and therefore undoubtedly the most astonishing of inventions.

This conclusion, however, would have been correct and plausible if the game of chess involved a predetermined process. Yet no move is the necessary outcome of any other move. Everything depends on the variable judgement of the players. Even assuming that the automaton's moves were themselves predetermined, they would inevitably be interrupted and disturbed by the non-predetermined will of its adversary.

*

It's freezing in this office, don't you find?

I'm going to call my assistant and in no time at all the person in charge of heating will come to adjust the thermostat.

Done.

Candice's efficiency is frightening. Right from her job interview I knew she was different from the others.

Hold on, I'll call her again on the intercom to ask her to come by to see us, since we're talking about her. I'm sure you'll love her.

My assistant steps into my office, all smiles. The documents that she's pressing against her chest rise and fall in time with her irregular breathing.

"Candice, you look exhausted. You take your work too seriously. Come over here so I can take your mind off it. Look at this picture. I've just had it framed. It dates back to when I was staying in the orphanage. It cost me a fortune, the rosewood."

"You're an orphan?"

"I haven't already told you that?"

She delicately shakes her skirt, as if to shoo away an insect. Something is bothering Candice, the static electricity perhaps. There are new products out on the market, fabulous aerosol sprays, that can take care of it.

I don't dare remark on her Chanel suit. I hold back, not wanting to appear too shallow. And I won't even mention her shoes, or her jacket collar, rabbit I believe, which adds a somewhat Nordic touch to the ensemble.

"Here, try to spot me."

"Professor, think about it, this photo must be as old as Methuselah."

"Come on, be a sport."

She accepts with a mischievous smile, pores over each orphan, hesitates, says nothing, eliminates people of colour, thereby neglecting the possibility that I might have faded over time.

She points to the boy I once was and lets out a sigh, as though touched by my past.

"Do you remember your classmates' names?"

"Only Montaigne Racine, the young Haitian rummaging in his nose behind me. Our teacher, Sister Marcella, harboured a keen dislike for him, despite the kindly air her cornette gives her in the picture."

*

Ever since I took up this appointment, I've dressed according to the principles of the Société des ambianceurs et des personnes élégantes (the Society of Ambiance-Makers and Elegant People), a.k.a. La Sape. But when I interview job applicants, I make an effort and put on the tie reserved for special occasions, the speckled silver and black one that I wear for magazine shoots.

La Sape is a popular sartorial club that originated in Cameroon in the early years of its independence. Its members, known as sapeurs, are patrons of the top couturiers. There are two types of sapeurs: those who refer to Enfant Mystère and those who adhere to the precepts of Feu Mamadou. The former, a very conservative set, are connoisseurs of the colours of fabrics and the seasons. The latter, forever captives of the baroque, wear garish colours.

The inventor of La Sape is believed to be Christian Loubaki, a.k.a. Enfant Mystère, a servant in the employ of Parisian aristocrats of the 16th *arrondissement*. He apparently started out with old clothes given to him by his employers. On returning to his native country, in collaboration with his old friend Hamadou Diop, he opened his first shop, La Saperie du Prince Loubaki.

It's sometimes said that La Sape indulges in the display of senseless abundance, in the exhibition of overpriced luxury attire, while Africa remains burdened with illiteracy, unemployment, and poverty. People say a lot of things. But how about some discernment?

*

There are moments when I replay Candice's job interview in my head. I see her entering my office and casting an amused glance at the objects on my desk, hear her declaring that the black marble bust of Poe gives my "hutch" character, and once again I feel ashamed, albeit briefly, for not knowing what a hutch is. How did we get by before dictionaries?

I ascribe my partiality for Candice to the subtle and quite charming flaw in her elocution, to her slender fingers, to her always slightly chipped nail polish.

Not five minutes after she walks through the door, I inform her that she's hired.

"It's not very complicated. You're the one who will write my novel. You'll earn a decent salary and will have the latest technological tools at your disposal. Of course, the key thing will be research."

Acting nonchalant, I turn toward the window and

point to the building that houses the punch-card computer purchased at great cost by the administration the year before, an entire floor to itself, just imagine.

*

My face goes numb more and more often. Whenever I get that sensation of pins and needles or of dysfunction, my eyes settle on the box where I keep the picture of the orphanage, and then I automatically think of Montaigne Racine, my friend and roommate.

I take out the photograph. There's Montaigne, second row, first on the left. He's ignoring the instructions of Sister Marcella, for whom this is no laughing matter.

"Press the palms of your hands together and, as you meditate, think about our Heavenly Father."

Instead of joining his hands together, Montaigne picks his nose. He's the only one who's aware of it, except for the photographer; the rest of us are too busy following Sister Marcella's instructions by posing like little angels for the camera.

Sitting in the front row, I don't see Montaigne disobeying.

*

Oftentimes, I get lost for hours in the contemplation of this picture. I'm especially captivated by the large fresco covering the back wall. The *sfumato* suggests the native Italy of the Sisters of the congregation. Forms and historical periods are jumbled together, but no one's going to make an issue of it. Art still has some future to look forward to.

Today, I'm walking in that fresco. The tall mountains, the peaceful lake, the little houses — all of it exudes a sense of calm and harmony. You would think this was Switzerland.

After a short stroll alongside a brook, I direct my gaze to the village in the left corner, and then I climb the promontory overlooking the marketplace, where vendors sell sausages named after the regional capital. Naples? Rome? Guess again.

Ambling among the stalls, I stop at one minded by a young woman, the daughter of a local wine grower. She tells me the last harvest was terrible; an individual with a strange complexion planted the vine shoots upside down. She recounts this unhappy incident in great detail but I'm unable to follow the thread, as if I were only half-listening, not entirely there. The wine grower's daughter notices and goes quiet. Then, seeing me walk away, she shouts, "Say hello to Hamadou!"

*

Sometimes when I stare for a long time at the picture
of the orphanage, my mind wanders off toward related
topics that I match up with certain generalities.

For example, earlier, I thought of Montaigne's
mother. By association, I became preoccupied with the
difficult task of naming as yet unborn children.

As they say, what's in a name?

Montaigne's mother, clearly a great reader, was
right on target, somewhat like that lady, born deaf, who
had christened her youngest Mozart. As for me, I find
it harder to christen my characters than my children.
Psychoanalysis could no doubt shed some light on this.

My eyes stay glued to the picture of the orphanage.
My gaze as a child, even the shape of my eyelids, is absolutely identical to my daughter Émilie's. I named her that
before she was born, in memory of the Emilian Way, the
ancient road connecting Piacenza to Modena, which I've
never taken.

*

I'm with Édouard one afternoon in 1975 at the Cinéma
Palace on rue Sainte-Catherine. We've come to see *Les
Ordres*, the film everyone is talking about. It's fiction but
has been made in the documentary style. The story is

about the arrest of five Québécois after the enactment of the War Measures Act on October 16, 1970, and, in particular, about the mental torture they undergo at the hands of the police before being released weeks later without a word of explanation.

In a very early scene in the film, the director, whom many critics regard as the world's best cameraman, points his lens at one of the leads. The actor introduces himself: "My name is Jean Lapointe, and in the film I am Clermont Boudreau. I was born on a farm and so was Marie. It seems to me that our biggest mistake was coming to the city. Right now, I'm working in the textile industry, and our hope is the union."

I often think of that moment when the actor becomes the character, and I wonder if Jean Lapointe feels it physically, the passage from one mode to the other.

My name is Alain Farah, and in this book I am Alain Farah.

*

I've been contemplating the picture of the orphanage for so long, examining it so closely, that I'm seeing double, sometimes even triple. It's not the mural in the refectory that absorbs me anymore, but Montaigne Racine, who multiplies and fidgets. He wants to speak with me.

We talk until nightfall.

For hours, he repeats the same thing, while telling me a thousand other things about it: you are the substance of your book.

*

Heading toward the washroom, I go by Candice's office. Even though it's late, she's perusing some bulky files. I interpret her look as a question. I stop.

"Professor, I came by to see you earlier this afternoon, but your door was shut. I heard you talking out loud for a long while. Would it be prying if I asked to whom you were speaking?"

"Oh, I was having a discussion with Montaigne Racine, the friend from the orphanage that you found so funny this morning. Well, believe it or not, he appeared to me."

"I'm quite willing to attribute some of your quirks to your eccentricity, but perhaps you're just overworked."

"Candice, fatigue and I are poles apart."

"My tasks include ensuring that you're performing at peak levels, that you maintain the same level of intensity, especially with all the discoveries I'm currently making. You ought to see Dr. Penfield, up at the top of rue University. He's developed a new consultation protocol."

"He sees people at this late hour, this Penfield?"

"Yes, until late into the night."

*

I believe Dr. Penfield's clinic is located east of rue University. Going up avenue McGregor along the McTavish reservoir, although I should turn right, I inexplicably turn left and, after walking for a few minutes, end up in front of the gate to a building I know all too well, the Allan Memorial Institute.

I walk toward the mansion-like building. A dwarf appears, as though out of thin air. Candice has really gone too far. Without saying a word, he gestures for me to follow him.

We enter the building. After climbing the black marble stairs, worn down in the middle, we arrive at the office of the homunculus on the top floor. The lighting in the room is very dim, but the city street lamps dissolve the shadows enough for me to find my way to the couch.

*

Born in Scotland, Hugh Allan, future shipping tycoon, future railroad promoter, future Sir, arrived in Montreal in 1826 and took a position as clerk with a grain merchant.

Thanks to his family and business connections, he moved into the naval construction sector after a few years and eventually became the owner of the most prodigious merchant fleet of the North Atlantic. His company, the

Allan Shipping Line, soon had the greatest loading capacity of all the companies operating out of Montreal, and by 1859 had become one of the most prosperous businesses in the province. And that was just the beginning. Allan went on to establish a permanent steamship line between Montreal and the British ports, thereby ensuring the shipment of cargo and increasing the number of immigrants coming from Europe.

During the 1860s, his accrued fortune made Allan the wealthiest person in Canada and incidentally enabled him to receive governors general, members of the royal family, and whatever the colony boasted in the way of big fish.

With eleven servants in his employ, including Christian Loubaki, a.k.a. Enfant Mystère, all that Sir Allan lacked was an estate. From the scions of Simon McTavish, that other Scot whom he would so admire, he bought a mansion on the slopes of mont Royal that surpassed in size and splendour all the residences existing in Canada at the time.

*

Thus, in 1863, Sir Hugh Allan commissioned from his architects the blueprints for the residence that, as my friend Umberto might say, would be the signifier of his power and wealth. Christened Ravenscrag, after a Scottish castle, the mansion, built in the Italian style, today still sits behind a stone wall at the top of rue McTavish.

The house, divided into several wings, has an asymmetrical façade dominated by an imposing tower that overlooks the main entrance. Inside, the design of each of the thirty-six rooms reflects a particular style. The hall and the dining room are in the Florentine style, the ballroom is in the French style, and the style of the library, with its oak panelling and heavily ornamented furniture, is decidedly Victorian.

Because the Allan family had a passion for breeding ravens, the fourteen-acre property was equipped with a vast aviary whose entrance was adorned with a sculpture representing this bird. After Sir Allan's death in 1882, his son Sir Montagu and his daughter-in-law inherited Ravenscrag. They enlarged the house to accommodate their four children and redecorated it. But then misfortune struck. Sir Allan's two granddaughters died in the wreckage of the *Lusitania*, and his two grandsons were killed in action during the First World War.

At Sir Montagu's death, Lady Allan donated Ravenscrag to the Royal Victoria Hospital and McGill University on the condition that the property should bear the name "Allan Memorial Institute," in memory of the four children who had died tragically.

In 1943, it was decided that the building would be transformed into a psychiatric hospital. The interior and exterior of the mansion underwent major changes that brought the building closer to the standards for asylums as conceived in the nineteenth century by the American architect Kirkbride, whose principles were followed in the construction of hundreds of psychiatric institutions throughout North America.

From that point on, things would not be the same at Ravenscrag. The great ballrooms where the English aristocracy had once gathered gave way to a new kind of living space where the mentally ill were no longer regarded as individuals to be excluded from society but as patients who deserved to bake cakes, play Ping-Pong, or sing together, under the inconspicuous and benevolent supervision of a few specialists.

*

For my part, I stretch out on the couch a few paces from the dwarf. I close my eyes and start the conversation good-humouredly, to ease the — it seems to me — rather grim atmosphere.

"Hello, Doctor…"

"Cameron."

"Yes, Dr. Cameroon… How do you do?"

"Cameron, not Cameroon. I don't look Scottish enough for you? Anyway, *comment allez-vous*? When one is in that seat, it usually means that something's the matter."

His voice is cavernous, mechanical, and intimidating, but I remain cordial.

"A friend appeared to me as I was scrutinizing a photograph. You know when you purposely cross your eyes while waiting for something to happen? It happened. The image of Montaigne began to move. I didn't intend to make a fuss over it, but Candice, my assistant, was worried, so I thought it best to come see you, the point being for my encounter with Montaigne not to hamper my research work."

"Yes, research, don't we all do that. What kind of work do you do?"

I answer, "Writer," and after a slight pause add, "I'm writing a novel in which a man entrusts a woman with the task of writing a novel instead of him, as he is clearly unable to do so because his mind is controlled by an intelligence agency."

I turn around to watch his reaction, curious to see the extent to which my project has impressed him. To my surprise, he appears on edge. He impatiently signals for me to return to my previous position. I comply but stay on the qui vive.

I hear him poking around in his drawer. After a long pause, he says, somewhat disdainfully, "The little you've told me indicates that you may be suffering from a mild form of insanity. Let me be frank: the options for treatment are limited. Here is your pillbox. Whenever you feel your thoughts taking a strange turn, take a capsule. Once you've swallowed it, everything should be back to normal within minutes."

I thank Dr. Cameron, whose terse style in no way affects his insight. I needed to utter only a few words for him to immediately diagnose my disorder, as if he were reading my thoughts.

*

As I leave the clinic, I see that wet snow has begun to fall and already the grounds of the former mansion have turned completely white. Rather than immediately returning to avenue des Pins, I choose to take a little stroll around Ravenscrag.

I focus my attention on the stone raven emerging from the building's keystone. I've read that the original owners used to breed this bird. This one looks angry; I avert my eyes, afraid to see the sculpture come alive, but then, realizing that my thoughts have taken a strange turn, I take out Dr. Cameron's pillbox, open it, pick out a capsule, place it on my tongue, collect all the saliva I have in my mouth, and swallow.

Standing in front of the raven, with my feet getting wetter and wetter, I itemize this protocol and record it mentally so that my description will be based on an intimate, lived experience.

★

Je me souviens.

The scene takes place last winter, in the late afternoon. The snowstorm absorbs all sound.

I've just written the first lines of my novel, so I allow myself a relaxing moment watching a science fiction series before my cousin calls to ask me to meet him at the garage.

When the phone rings, I'm in intergalactic space. Édouard says, "Listen, we won't be able to fix the Italian's car tonight. I have to go to Ravenscrag. My father isn't feeling well."

"Nothing serious, I hope?"

"I have no idea. I can't get through to anyone."

"I'm on my way."

★

It's been a long time since I last saw Nab. To know he's lying motionless in his room surrounded by fake plants, pictures of his past life, press clippings praising the invention of his revolutionary lamp — it all makes me want to cry.

Édouard and I have agreed to meet in front of the Ravenscrag gate. It's still snowing, just as it will be a year on when I go out after my consultation with Dr.

Cameron. I'm muddling up the chronology; Candice will resent that, but the climate's out of joint and it isn't the only one. The sidewalks are slippery. We take baby steps as we continue up the hill.

I say to Édouard, "Have you learned anything more?"

"I imagine his new treatment is wearing him out."

After entering the mansion, we charge up a large black marble stairway. We hear cries. The door opens. Édouard's mother flings herself at him, repeating all the while, "He's dead, he's dead."

*

Even though it breaks the rhythm of the story just when, according to Candice, something like an inciting incident is in progress, here is a capsule portrait of Édouard, my first cousin and son of Nab, the youngest brother of Yolande, my mother.

Édouard was born three days after me, in the same hospital: the Royal Victoria, on the McGill University campus in Montreal. We've always been inseparable, mainly because my mother and his father were very close, having lost their own father, whose given name was Édouard, in tragic circumstances, when my mother was twelve and Nab hardly six years old.

Édouard is a mechanic, I write books — it's the same thing. I've always lived in apartments with a garage, which my cousin would use to practice automobile mechanics while I wasted my time reading novels and smoking electronic cigarettes.

When I was very small, alone in my bed at night, I would worry myself sick at the thought that one day Édouard would die. The prospect so terrified me that I would wet my bed.

*

If a Haitian invited me, on a stormy night, into a gloomy mansion and offered me not a blue capsule or a red capsule but an ordinary, healthy family rather than an insane family, I wouldn't hesitate for even a moment — I would not change my story in any way. Even though my wish to transform it — the story — is what prompts me to write.

What would I have become without my family?

An accountant, an engineer, a psychiatrist, any number of things, no doubt, but never a writer of books.

One stormy night when I was watching TV, comfortably stretched out on my French terry loveseat, I stumbled on *The Ed Sullivan Show*. Among the various entertainers on the program, one of them stood out from the crowd with his little gangland boss look. He made a strong impression on me. He was a Michigan-born crooner, a guy named Marshall Mathers. In fact, on a sheet of paper that I stuck on my refrigerator with a magnet, I transcribed a verse of the number he had performed for the talk-show audience: *Now I would never diss my own momma just to get recognition / Take a second to listen for who you think this record is dissing.*

*

As I was saying, Nab is dead.

Édouard and I stay with his mother for a long while to comfort her. She is inconsolable, but she eventually collects herself and calms down. She explains that, over the past few days, Nab had complained to the nurses of chest pains. His symptoms worsened in the early morning, he began to vomit violently, and his doctor was slow to react. Édouard's mother dozed off at her husband's bedside; Nab's heart stopped beating without her realizing. My cousin and I arrived minutes later.

Nab is before us, in his bed. I don't understand when people say, "He has gone to sleep," in reference to someone's death. Nab does not appear to be asleep; he is staring blankly, his mouth half-open, and on his unshaven, livid face I read horror. I'm tempted to take his hand, but I don't dare touch him. His colour frightens me, and I'm afraid his body is already cold.

Her eyes still red, Édouard's mother turns toward me. She wants me to break the news to my mother: *It falls to you to tell her, even though you haven't spoken in years.*

It's true, I have a troubled history with my mother. She lost me when I was still a child.

With some difficulty, I manage to leave Ravenscrag, with its architecture of thirty-six doors arrayed on either side of a long central corridor, none of which leads out of the building, as if one had to agree to invent a thirty-seventh in order to exit.

*

Walking in the snowstorm, I hail a taxi and give the driver my mother's address.

In the car, I ponder the way to announce her brother's death, speaking out loud to find the right words, raising my voice so I can hear myself above the music of Radio Caraïbes that the driver is playing at maximum volume.

The right words don't come. Oh well, I'll improvise.

*

When my mother opens the door, I note how she recoils.

"What are you doing here? I was told you were studying in Europe."

"Nab has had an attack. I've come to let you know. I didn't want to tell you over the phone."

"Is it serious?"

"I don't know."

"What's the matter?"

"It's not clear. Put on your coat, we'll go see him."

"Are you crazy, in this storm? What's the hurry?"

"It would be good if we went right now."

"Are you keeping something from me?"

"What do you mean?"

"You would tell me if it was serious, wouldn't you?"

"I don't know."

"What do you mean?"

"I believe it's quite serious."

"It's over? Tell me if it's over."

I give her the look that says, "It's over."

*

I'll cut here, before my mother's reaction. One might say I'm leaving her off camera, but it's actually an editing effect, to be read not as something done out of a sense of decency, but as the recognition of failure that comes whenever I write. Literature simply doesn't measure up to life.

In reality, when I inform my mother of her brother's death, she begins to moan. I stand frozen in front of her, especially because she interrupts her lamentations with the word *baba*—"*baba, baba*," she repeats—an Arab term of endearment used when speaking to one's father.

At the funeral parlour, three days later, the prattle

of an old aunt enlightens me as to the reason for this repeated *"baba."* Édouard, my mother's father, died on December 8, the same day as Nab, fifty years earlier. When I rang the doorbell, my mother had been haunted since morning by that anniversary. On seeing me show up at her house after all those years to announce her brother's death, she cracked. Something in time collapsed. Overcome by the confusion of time periods, my mother became a child once again asking for her father, as one does in moments of despair.

The year was 1962. For my mother, it was 1912.

★

All parents will tell you: explaining to your child that death exists is fraught with peril. Standing by Nab's remains, my daughter asked me if we too were going to die one day. I tried to explain that life was of limited duration; we're born and then we die.

"Everyone's going to die, Dad? Even Mom?"

"Yes, Émilie, everyone dies. One day, all human beings living on earth today will have disappeared. Does that worry you?"

"No, because that's when the dinosaurs will come back."

*

It seems complicated, but it's simple. I haven't lost my way. I hired Candice, I gave her a demanding assignment, she experienced anxiety, she projected her symptoms onto me, and I ended up in front of Cameron, in front of Ravenscrag with the snow absorbing all sound.

Here I am again, feet frozen, motionless in the storm. And a Haitian night watchman, wearing a suit in line with the standards of La Sape, is approaching, flashlight in hand. You or I would do the same. A man in the wee hours staring at a stone raven and smoking an electronic cigarette — something is amiss.

I can recognize a disciple of La Sape from miles away. This watchman is a master at applying the foundational principles of the society, including the sacrosanct rule of the Trilogy. Three colours for an ensemble, not one more, not one less. Dressing in accordance with the principles of La Sape means knowing how to display flamboyant arrangements: a three-piece Dior suit with Weston crocodile shoes, why not. It's showing off your white merino wool tailcoat, your McQueen tie, your mahogany pipe, your cane with a "system" that includes, in the handle or the shaft, a compartment for storing cutlery, sometimes a weapon. Being a good sapologist involves exploring fabrics, patterns, accessories; it's about understanding how to live the experience of a garment.

"Can I help you, sir? I suppose you are here for the enigma of Bologna?"

"Actually, I work on the far side of the reservoir. I lost my way—it's so foolish—after I left the clinic. I was contemplating that stone raven jutting out from the keystone."

"For two hours? Admit that you were hypnotized by Ravenscrag... Quite a building, isn't it? It is said that Sir Allan had his mansion built on the mountain so he could keep an eye on his fleet at all times."

"And this famous enigma?"

"The enigma of Bologna... They have been attempting to solve it for centuries. Scores of cryptologists have come up short. In any case, I hope you are not upset that I stopped to question you. It is part of the new security procedure established by Dr. Cameron after the death of one of his patients. If you only knew how many suspicious individuals I catch loitering around the mansion each night. And it has gotten worse ever since the boss began recruiting students for his hydrotherapy experiments. The young people try to sneak into Ravenscrag's indoor swimming pool."

"Ravenscrag's indoor swimming pool?"

"You are not aware of it, naturally. It serves in the treatment of Dr. Cameron's patients. Outside the treatment hours, the institute's doctors go there to lounge about. I dare say, at the risk of appearing vulgar, I understand them very well, with all the lovely creatures climbing out of the water."

"What do you mean?"

"The show starts during the free swim, when the nurses — pretending to be ingénues in their prettiest bathing suits — come to join the doctors. There are even girls wearing those new things: bikinis. Needless to say, I spend my time making sure that everything is safe, and I have no qualms about using force if I have any doubts about some of the nurses."

By way of reply, I give him a quick, embarrassed smile. Almost imperceptibly, through a combination of civilities and witticisms, I swiftly usher the conversation to its conclusion: fascinating, but I have a meeting with my assistant, my socks are soaking wet, I must run, see you again.

*

I arrive at the office before dawn throws its sinister rosy fingers over the horizon. There's a surprise waiting for me: Candice is already there, unless she never left. Pinned to the wall in front of her, newspaper clippings and various sheets of papers bearing peculiar notes (Lysergic acid? MK-Ultra? Page-Russell Method?) are all connected with string, forming a vast constellation of invisible links.

"So, Candice, the investigation — any progress?"

"You'll have my report tomorrow first thing in the morning. You won't be disappointed. It's big. Bigger than you thought."

Leaning against the doorpost, I scan the items on the wall. How tiresome! Too many words. But she does cut a terrific figure in that pantsuit.

"Is that Chanel?"

"Excuse me?"

The curtness of her response sends us both back to our respective roles. I straighten up, check my Double Windsor and, just before leaving, I ask, "And the novel?"

"Oh, that. That's different. I'm faced with a number of problems. I'd like to talk to you about it."

"That won't be necessary, Candice. Do what you feel is right."

Content with the way things are going, I return to my dear office untroubled by worries, knowing that, in the life of a writer, insouciance and thoughtlessness are fleeting sentiments.

In the middle of the afternoon, on my couch, I try to take a short nap and assume a semi-fetal position. I look for the right posture, the exact rate of breathing, but to no avail. I'm constantly disturbed by the telephone ringing, colleagues knocking on the door. I have to get up repeatedly. I make a show of good humour to their faces, while hiding my load of anxieties.

I decide to devote myself to inconsequential pursuits.

Having dusted my objects, I set about arranging my books in alphabetical order (Adorno, Condon, Duras, Pellerin, Rimbaud), then according to the order in which I read them (Condon, Pellerin, Duras, Rimbaud, Adorno), then by nationality (American: Condon; French: Duras, Rimbaud; French-Canadian: Pellerin; German: Adorno).

As the day wears on, my symptoms manifest: I feel pins and needles in my face, not knowing if the cause is a pinched nerve or blood vessel or a needle; I'm more aware than usual of the presence of my teeth in my mouth even though they aren't grinding; I have a stomach ache; I don't hear the voices in my head anymore, but their silence terrifies me.

After completing the inventory of my ailments, I note that I've just had my first sleepless night. The course of events is becoming murky. There's a price to pay for every unsuccessful nap.

*

Even an endless day ends up coming to an end. It's about time. I leave the office, taking the back way out of the building for the simple pleasure of walking along the McTavish reservoir. The sun is going down behind mont Royal, bathing the environs in an unreal light.

In the 1930s, the reservoir's little lake of potable water was not yet covered over. During the outings allowed by the orphanage, we would go there, Montaigne and I, to play with boats remotely controlled through electromagnetic waves. I never won a race, but I enjoyed imagining the speedboats at real regattas.

The lake was a resort area in the very heart of the city. A beautiful thing with a practical function.

Since then, things have changed. For safety and hygiene reasons, the authorities decided to introduce a bylaw and, in keeping with the new measures, a small plateau was created over the lake, which was sealed with a concrete slab. Fortunately, people still go there to picnic on sunny days.

In the summer, I'm fond of going by there to see young families playing with kites, coloured balls, Frisbees. Occasionally, if a drizzle deigns to refresh me, I think back to my afternoons with the Huguenot woman, before things went awry.

*

Was I going to discuss love?

No, I was going to discuss city planning.

Montreal has several reservoirs of drinking water, including the McTavish Station, located right by the McGill University campus, at the foot of mont Royal. The reservoir, dug in 1856, was initially a lake with a capacity of fourteen million gallons. That's a great deal of water. Over the years it was enlarged a number of times.

The elegant pumping station is reminiscent of a medieval castle and is in perfect harmony with the adjacent elements of the McGill campus and Royal Victoria Hospital. The masonry, stairways, front steps, doors, windows, slate roofs, and copper flashing—it all looks splendid.

Inside, there are twelve massive pumps that draw water up from the Saint-Laurent, the water is then redistributed by gravity throughout the surrounding neighbourhoods.

The McTavish reservoir was sealed with a concrete slab because it was feared that the patients at the Royal Victoria might contaminate it and vice versa. The slab was then covered with a lawn abutting avenue McGregor, which, in 1978, would be renamed avenue du Docteur-Penfield, in homage to Dr. Cameron's perennial rival. As for Dr. Penfield's neurological clinic, to get there one need only turn right when McGregor reaches avenue des Pins. It's all so well designed that one would have to make an effort to get lost. Indeed.

*

For the time being, I know where I am—on avenue des Pins—and as it happens I bump into Umberto, who is coming out of a student residence, proud as a peacock.

"My my, *amico mio*, you're so pale. What's the matter?"

"Well, I've just had a sleepless night."

"And it's no doubt to make sure you have two sleepless nights in a row that chance has made our paths cross, don't you think? Come, follow me, I'm on my way to boulevard Dorchester."

"You've got tickets for the inauguration? How do you manage to get invited everywhere?"

"An architect that I was involved with. She wants to introduce me to a bunch of people, to show that she has good contacts in the Italian intelligentsia. I've got two passes. You can come with me. There will be some wonderful women to take your mind off your Swiss lady. Learn to have some fun, *bello*. Do as I do. Just look at how I thrive whenever I'm in Montreal."

"And what does Mrs. Eco think of your American jaunts?"

He doesn't appreciate my comments but knows me well enough not to worry. We continue walking in silence, at least until avenue du Parc, where workers are putting the final touches on the new concrete interchange that will be opened in a few days. Umberto resumes the conversation as if I'd never mentioned his wife.

"I still haven't settled with your cousin for the repair work on the big American car I shipped to Italy."

"You know, ever since his father died, Édouard is having trouble staying on top of his accounts."

"Lucky for me!"

"As ethical as ever..."

"You can get down off your high Catholic horse. Death, women, cash, it all goes together. If you want to succeed with your books, you need to understand this. Think of what Montaigne said: you are the substance of your book."

Hearing these words from Umberto makes me feel ill, so I swallow a capsule on the sly.

*

Duras, in *Écrire*, deplores that too many books are lacking in freedom. She admonishes writers for acting like cops, whereas writing is a breeding ground for delinquents. By being content with conformist little books, scribblers take pleasure in their own neutralization, they make books with no night, pastime books, books for travelling, not books that sink into the mind, not books that speak the dark grief of all life.

*

I met Umberto when I was studying in Europe. I like him, but the exuberance of his personality grates on me, not to mention his books, riddled with metaphors, where he spends fifteen pages marvelling at the doorway of a medieval church.

But aside from his writing quirks and the ease with which he puts my moral convictions to the test, Umberto is important for me. I use him to experience interesting things.

★

I can't believe that instead of going to bed to catch up on my sleep so I can be in good shape for my meeting with Candice tomorrow morning, I'm going out on the town with the Italian.

I can't believe it because it's not true.

Just like me, Umberto does not exist. I drew the outline of this character from a rather funny incident in the summer of 2007.

Léa-Catherine, an old schoolmate who, after studying architecture in Venice, had decided to settle in Italy, was back in Montreal on vacation for a few weeks.

She invited me to a barbecue that she was throwing in her mother's garden. It was a pleasant evening, and I was making small talk with Capucine, a shy, pretty brunette, when a guy interrupted our conversation to openly put the make on her.

The contents of his seductive discourse moved me.

Without any obvious reason, he began to describe Eco's work to Capucine, stressing its complexity and the need to read it in the original language to understand the realities of Italy.

The guy's spiel ended with a comment about the Emilia-Romagna region, which had begun to obsess me. So much so that in *Matamore no 29*, the novel I was then writing, I peppered the narrative, without knowing why, with references to the city of Bologna, whose name designates a mortadella so finely ground it appears homogeneous, with no visible trace of the assorted bits from which it's made: pork snouts, rooster feet, beef anuses.

★

I unobtrusively swallow a capsule, then a second, and a third.

Here we are at the party. People are quietly waiting in line to go inside but there is some jostling going on nonetheless. They're excited to be part of this evening, understandably so. Place Ville Marie is being inaugurated — no small event.

In the great hall, the hostess gives me a strange look. To avoid arousing suspicion, I tell her, "I'm from another era."

We've hardly stepped inside when Umberto starts to pick out the beautiful women: "You'd think this was a scene from Fellini's latest film, right?"

I make an effort to examine their legs and chests, but the truth is I'm incapable of judging them solely on the basis of appearance. My detachment irritates Umberto.

"Oh, come on, you're no fun. Find a woman you like, and I'll chat her up for you."

While he says this, he continues to sweep his eyes across the room. I give in to his insistence.

"At the far end of the room, the one with her back to us, with the black hat. I like her."

"But you can't even see her face. And her pillbox hat is ridiculous. We're surrounded by all these lovely little faces and you settle on the girl with her back turned? You depress me."

"She's the one I must talk to," I answer earnestly.

"Well, if it will improve your mood..."

*

Umberto heads toward the back of the hall and along the way brushes a waitress's posterior. He touches the woman with the pillbox hat, who immediately swings around.

On seeing her face, I'm gripped by a strange sensation. I feel uneasy, but artificially, by which I mean that the sensation hits me without being announced by anxiety; it comes out of nowhere.

I try to calm down by thinking about the swallowed capsules, and then I take two more, to be certain. At least Umberto won't be able to criticize my choice. Silly hat or not, the woman is stunning.

As a rule, I don't like tall women. From the very first, I can see the imbalance in the eventual wedding picture. Whatever dwarfs may say, I don't like it when the man is shorter.

I can't keep my eyes off her, this black-haired woman. Her dress, at once fitted and puffed at the shoulders, makes her a dead ringer for Sean Young, who plays the replicant in the film *Blade Runner*. The makeup around her eyes has been meticulously applied, but owing to the distance between us I'm unable to verify the response of her iris so as to determine if this is a robot. Her complexion is pale but not transparent; the veins in her face are invisible. I'm reassured. I loathe whatever blurs the surface.

*

What is beauty? The question has nagged me ever since I first found a woman to my liking.

One day, on coming home from school, I sat down in front of the television. Clicking away at the Jerrold, I stumbled on a leggy spy in an episode of a Japanese cartoon series. This triggered an upheaval in my psychology.

For the rest of my life I would seek that overall feeling of enthrallment at the vital force that takes hold of me when I like a woman. What I find odd today is that to regain that marvellous feeling of keeping company with beauty in its absence, I must focus on a specific manifestation of it: a dishevelled braid, a gleaming eye, a generous or delicate bosom.

I could expand the list until all my female readers have recognized themselves, but that would be manipulative. Still, an impish smile, teeth misaligned just the right amount, a Swiss accent, some slight speech defect, refined makeup—all of it, for all time, unsettles me, troubles me.

*

That's why I can discuss makeup for hours, perhaps not as eloquently as Baudelaire, but with a degree of expertise. When I was twenty I had a summer job at the Sephora on the Champs-Élysées, the largest in Europe, to pay for my studies in literature. Since then, I analyze how the women I bump into use makeup. I do this as an aesthete, though I may on occasion grab someone's ass.

The mascara of young, inexperienced women, sometimes light, always defining, mascara that lends depth and a unique quality to the gaze, enables a woman to appear magical and supernatural: she who astonishes, she who charms, she who adorns herself to be adored, she who borrows from every art the means to transcend nature, to conquer hearts and capture imaginations.

Purists rail against the imposture, as if there were such a thing as natural beauty, as if this business of authenticity was anything but hogwash.

Who cares if the subterfuge and artifice are public knowledge, when the effect is irresistible? Makeup artfully applied creates the illusion of a life that surpasses life.

★

This woman whom I've unwittingly chosen from among all the others frightens me with her beauty.

She knows that I'm looking at her, so she looks at me, and as soon as I turn toward her she averts her head. I swallow a capsule and sit down next to Umberto, who places his hand on the woman's thigh just as she lets her eyes settle on me once again. This time she stares at me.

Umberto grows bolder. Moving his hand toward her crotch, he declares, "You know, miss, I am a semiologist specialized in medieval scholasticism. I recently published *Sviluppo dell'estetica medievale*, and I am also interested in the avant-garde, which includes my friend right here" — he points at me. "I am in the process of finishing an essay on the subject; the only thing missing is the title."

Without missing a beat, the woman suggests "The Open Work." Energized by the suggestion, Umberto continues, "I am about to be appointed to a prestigious position in Emilia-Romagna, a region of my country, a very pretty one, especially if you like the mountains."

I can feel my face going numb again, and it's getting colder and colder in here. I take another capsule and then interrupt Umberto's smooth talk.

"I think I'm coming down with something. I ought to get going."

"What are you saying, *carissimo*? I thought you wanted to have experiences! At least let me introduce you ... Actually, would you tell me just your first name ..."

The woman stands up and straightens her skirt. Even though Umberto is the one who asked, she directs her reply to me.

"Salomé."

My fingers tighten around the little box in my pocket, but before I have a chance to take another capsule she tells me, "I didn't expect to see you here. Your books are so harshly critical of society life."

I'm amazed she recognizes me. It's happened only once before, at the Home Depot in Sainte-Foy. Despite my shivering, I try to answer something witty, and we begin to chat. Umberto withdraws, passing behind the young woman. He silently mouths words of encouragement.

★

The conversation very quickly shifts from banter to more sombre subjects. The young woman expresses a good deal of interest in me and takes the liberty of making an annoying remark: "You write like someone who had no childhood. You bear a grudge against your mother, don't you?"

"Don't be so presumptuous. You've read my books, but everything I say in them is false. You know nothing about me other than my name. We're on the same footing: your first name is Salomé, and it will take a little more than that for me to lose my head."

"Do you often allude to the Gospel when speaking with women?"

A waiter offers me some appetizers on a silver platter: veal and artichoke balls flavoured with orange and tarragon, stuffed mushrooms, a raspberry sardine focaccia. I choose the *accras de morue* but wait before taking a bite: once burned, twice shy.

"I must admit that I have always found the episode of John the Baptist's beheading disturbing."

"What does it tell you?"

"That a kiss could kill if beauty is not death."

Then I bite into the appetizer. I could have sworn it was cod, but the texture suggests queen crab. And the hint of cayenne is not bad either.

"Is that an invitation? It's rare for a man to admit to a passion for women of the castrating kind, but in your case, wouldn't that make sense? Given your problems with your mother... A bleak childhood produces good writers. That's what you claim to be, isn't it?"

"I'm only interested in such women if I can castrate them in turn. Apart from that, I'm prepared to go quite far."

"Is that a challenge? Actually, what is the title of the book you're writing now?"

"Writing? Writing is a big word. As if I were actually the one writing! *Nevermore* it's called. I wasn't intending to discuss it, but the further I get, the more I realize that my book deals with my illness."

"If you like, I can be your cure."

Salomé steps closer. I'm now fully aware of her magnetism, the danger laid bare by her black widow charisma. I venture to wrap my arm around her waist; she smiles approvingly. The servers stop interrupting us, and the guests in the great hall move away, unless it's the other way around. I let my hands wander over Salomé's dress, I touch her ribs. She moves even closer, places her hand on my shoulder, and kisses me on the neck.

*

My mind is in overdrive. I search for a punch line to break the spell, but the wave of panic returns. My thoughts spawn images that don't exist; the action shifts unpredictably in time and space. It's hard to describe. The place that serves as a backdrop to the scene remains unchanged — this is September 13, 1962, Place Ville Marie is being inaugurated on September 13, 1962 — but I have the impression, despite knowing that we're not moving, that Salomé is leading me to the washroom, that we're experiencing a moment of high intensity, that from afar Umberto sees me but doesn't understand what's going on. I have the impression that everything is becoming sexual.

And yet, nothing happens.

I'm in the room with the big fish, Salomé kisses me, and then whispers in my ear as she hands me a package, "I will be your cure."

She moves away and disappears into the crowd. I decide to leave too. It's all well and good to enjoy life, but I have no plans to go insane. As I leave the reception, I turn around just once and see Umberto, now busy entertaining two tall Slavic women who have defected to the West, giving me a disappointed look.

★

After a long taxi ride through the city, during which I wincingly swallow at least three capsules, I come home and make myself a bowl of cereal, having first opened the package given to me by Salomé and flipped through the contents: a book by a certain Carrère entitled *I Am Alive and You Are Dead*.

I sit down in front of the television without switching it on.

Thanks to a few breathing exercises, I recover my senses and am finally able to press the buttons on the Jerrold. I say to myself that it would be nice to stumble on a badly translated Japanese sci-fi series. But there's something else on.

Near the shore is a white house with an overhanging terrace whose balustrade calls to mind the Rome of the emperors. The interior of the villa is visible through the picture window, and the camera surprises two lovers kissing.

My attention is focused on the woman, a singer at the peak of fame, adulated and awash with riches, talked about in the newspapers every day.

There is movement: the lovers go out onto the terrace.

The woman's celebrity is such that as soon as she steps outside the villa, she is assailed by a frenzied barrage of flashes.

Perhaps the reporters want to photograph the tattoo on the inside of her left arm, a quote from Rilke in gothic letters: "Go into yourself. Find out the reason that commands you to write; see whether it has spread its roots into the very depths of your heart; confess to yourself whether you would have to die if you were forbidden to write."

*

The camera draws away from the tattoo and alights on the lover who is speaking to the woman in Italian (Umberto translates):

"*Hai fiducia in me?*" (Do you trust me?)

"*Ovviamente!*" (Of course!)

The image suggests that the action is coming to us through the photographer's lens, as though form itself were beginning to speak to us.

But something unexpected occurs. The lovers quarrel, and the man orders the woman to look at the camera.

Is he in league with Paparazzo?

I concentrate very hard on the action to grasp its hidden significance, but it's no use, the meaning grows more opaque.

Suddenly, the woman breaks a bottle of champagne over the lover's head and, out of revenge, he pushes the woman over the terrace.

She falls falls falls with a black-and-white spiral in the background, somewhat like the opening of *Vertigo*, the Hitchcock film I saw with Édouard at the Cinéma Le Dauphin. Could this be another story about a woman who returns from the realm of the dead?

*

The woman continues to fall until she smashes her head on the ground.

There's blood everywhere. She's dead — that is indisputable. And yet, she's not. I knew it; I feel that I'm witnessing a scene from *Vertigo*, even if Kim Novak is less disturbing than Stefani Germanotta.

She emerges from a limousine in a wheelchair, wearing a lapis lazuli neck brace; it's unlike anything I've ever seen, despite my coming from an injury-prone family.

Her removable, retractable sunglasses are at the cutting edge of optometry. She lifts a lens, keeps her right eye hidden and plays the one-eyed woman, like the devil.

Strains of catchy music can be heard and, after a few notes, a team of stretcher-bearers from out of nowhere begins to undress the woman.

One can see her ample bust, her long legs. It's exciting even though I'm at a loss: usually Stefani has small breasts and short legs. I look more closely. She's covered with metal, especially her head; you might think that, like

Sir Allan's grandson, she was in the Great War and the missing pieces of skull have been replaced by iron plates.

I believe the term used in such cases is trepanation.

*

I want to turn off the TV, but I also want to not turn it off.

The trepanned woman, whose metal plates have gone from grey to gold as if Midas were the on-duty surgeon, now initiates the dance of the dead.

I saunter through this morgue of images, the pictures come alive, I'm racked with fear.

I swallow a capsule and then another. I think about Salomé.

A kiss would kill if beauty were not death.

I see a dead woman in a bath, drained of her blood, her mechanical ears made from the same metal as the head of the trepanned woman. I distinguish another who wears a diamond eye mask, blood streaming from her mouth, and still another, sprawled on a *récamier*, eviscerated, her chest crawling with maggots.

I swallow a third capsule. Perhaps I should check to see how many are left in my pillbox.

I don't.

Walking in the woods, while there's no wolf skulking about, I come across a tall blond woman lying on the ground, a plastic bag covering her head. Has no one told her she would suffocate? Her legs are spread wide, which ordinarily should make you fear the worst. I fear the worst.

I start running to warn someone but find myself before a series of thirty-six doors that open onto a series of thirty-six dead women.

A golden substance seeps from each of their mouths, possibly honey.

I enter the white house with the large overhanging terrace. At my feet, the brains of the servant are soaking in a red puddle. The servant has been pushed down the great circular stairway, her skull shattered.

I go out by the garden only to find another dead woman on the lawn, curled up next to a shovel. What is she doing there? We'll never know, not about her and not about the others.

*

But it goes on. The legs of a woman cut in half appear, the feet wearing yellow stiletto heels.

In the next frame, I'm lying in a four-poster bed, a blond at my side, alive this time, open-mouthed. She's holding an empty box of medicine in her hand. Bad omen.

In a large room I see a man, and I recognize the famous singer's lover; he has my face, every last feature the same. Except that he has lost an eye, though this doesn't prevent him from leafing through the newspaper, which, however, doesn't mention the victims of the dance of the dead.

The door opens and the singer appears. She has come back to avenge the vengeance. Dressed as Minnie Mouse, she wears dark glasses. I ask her for some elderberry water. I have no idea what it tastes of. It's British, I believe.

She smiles. *"Hai gusti aristocratici..."* (You have aristocratic tastes.)

Despite her remark she serves me obediently, even dropping a few ice cubes in my glass. What I don't see is that she is not at all obedient; she surreptitiously sprinkles a powder on my drink that makes it fizz.

I freeze.

She places her hand in front of her face in a way that signifies "oops," and then she makes a call on her nail-phone.

Is that possible?

Yes, everything is possible, here.

I listen closely as she confesses to the investigator. Narrating her own crime, she invents a new breed of criminal.

Night falls. The police investigation gets underway. The investigation progresses.

The woman is charged with murder; her fingerprints were found on her sunglasses.

I'm writing a nightmare, living a nightmare.

I switch off the TV. Now I'm even more anxious than I was when I came back from the inauguration. I swallow one last capsule and go to bed.

*

I toss in my bed incessantly, my body itches because of the fatigue, I'm cold, I rub my feet together under the covers.

I'm coming down with something.

I hear my breath, and I try to quiet my thoughts down, to pace them to the rhythm of my breathing. I'm not getting enough oxygen, my face is growing numb, I nearly call Édouard for assurance.

Why did Salomé offer to become my cure?

I look out the window of my room through the little hole punched out in the blind. The sky has shed some of its darkness—this is terrible, dawn is breaking.

I detest this moment; something always gets spoiled. Often, at daybreak, I recall a statement made by an old art history teacher, whom I can still hear telling us, as he stood in front of the screen where he'd projected slides of paintings by Géricault and Caravaggio, "There are painters of the night, like Rembrandt and de La Tour. But there are very few painters of dawn, painters of the murky light."

Fortunately, it's winter. The birds won't start singing.

I'm not cut out to go without sleep.

What's the use of staying in bed if I'm not resting?

I get up, no need to have another breakfast. Shirt, meeting-day tie, Double Windsor, I'm off.

*

Before arriving at McGill I say to myself, well, now that I've spotted him in the distance, why not go the long way around and say hello to the watchman who questioned me yesterday morning.

He's still wearing a garishly coloured suit: emerald jacket, fuchsia shirt, poppy ascot, burgundy trousers. Nice work, but the watchman is overzealous: I count four colours. Oddly, his skin seems less black than before, especially at the hairline, as if he were a Caucasian in blackface. It really does look like makeup for a minstrel show, those early nineteenth-century American perform-ances where white actors, their faces blackened with shoe polish, made fun of Afro-Americans by portraying them as simpletons whose only talents were for music and dance.

I keep my anxiety from showing. I hide my belief that one must at all times be on the idiots' side rather than on the side of clever people, and I greet the Haitian, who replies, "I have done some research on you, Professor, in the computer's central database. So, you like books to the point of writing them? Do you know that Edgar Poe stayed at Ravenscrag in the nineteenth century? Actually, the mansion belonged to the brother of his adoptive father. The latter no doubt felt that a trip far from New England would be beneficial for the poet, who was beginning to take too great an interest in liquor, gambling, and women."

"Poe lived in this neighbourhood? I'll tell Candice to slip something about that into my book."

"Oh, yes, one more thing. I have made arrangements with Miss Cameron, the boss's daughter, to allow you to use the indoor swimming pool. If I am not the one minding the door, just mention my name to my colleague, and he will let you in without any formalities."

"And your name is?"

"For you it is Hamadou, Hamadou Diop."

For me? What does he mean by that? His facial expression makes it clear that he won't elaborate, and I resume my walk along avenue des Pins, toward McGregor. Next time I'll bring my swimsuit.

*

No sooner do I arrive than Candice snaps at me: "You haven't forgotten our meeting, Professor?"

Candice has changed from her pantsuit into more

casual attire: sweater, cigarette pants, footwear midway
between pumps and t-strap shoes. I notice her blond hair
nonchalantly gathered up in a chignon, the coil sitting on
her head, and her eyes, livened up with kohl. I believe the
appropriate term is cat eye makeup. I'm not surprised,
knowing that Candice has three of them, cats that is: a
black, a grey, and a ginger one.

"Of course not. I've even donned my special tie."

"I have a few things to tell you. I've made a good deal
of headway in my research."

"Okay, but first let me take off my coat."

A moment later, just as in the movies, I flop down
into my armchair, lean back so that my feet no longer
touch the floor, start when my chair suddenly tilts back
but pretend the tilt is part of the choreography. I light
an electronic cigarette and, in speaking to my assistant,
slowly articulate each syllable: "Close the door, Candice.
I'm listening."

My assistant leaves my office a half hour later, satis-
fied that she's done her duty but also worried that she's
provided me with more good reasons to go mad.

Some damn fine work... In sum, the CIA is not just
interested in our thoughts; the agency is on the verge of
controlling us remotely.

The war is changing, the theatre of operations is
moving. The assault on the mind henceforward is far
more devastating than the one aimed at the body. If I'm

to escape from our enemies, if I'm to make it through, I'll need a thousand Vietnams.

*

But to truly understand, we must return to the past. Have you noticed that tragic destinies always work according to the same principle? By desperately fleeing from whatever threatens us, we rush toward it even more swiftly. The story of Giuseppe Nozze is no exception, and Candice was categorical in this regard: that is where it all started.

At the start of the Second World War, this Canadian of Italian background served in the Allied forces with the rank of sergeant.

A man whose parents had left Naples in the hope of finding a better world in North America.

A man who had gone to the best Catholic schools.

A man who ended up in a unit whose mission was to recapture the Emilia-Romagna region from the Duce's troops.

This seemingly simple operation became complicated despite Nozze's reconnoitring. The sergeant had rented a small furnished apartment in the suburbs of Bologna, passing himself off as the biographer of Racine (or Corneille or Montaigne, I can't recall).

During the assault on the capital, Nozze's contingent

was kidnapped and his unit was reported missing for several days.

Having heard no news, the soldiers' wives, imagining the worst, grieved and made funeral arrangements.

Then, from one day to the next, the soldiers resurfaced, safe and sound.

At least, so it seemed.

*

The enemy had agreed to set them free just like that, without asking anything in return?

It's bizarre, I'll grant you that, but at first the families were so relieved to have their sons back that no one pointed out this aberration. Yet it doesn't take a degree in polemology to understand that this liberation covered up a horrendous truth.

Some time after the soldiers' return, the captain of the mission—later played by Sinatra in one of the two films that Hollywood would make about the incident—recommended that Nozze be awarded the Governor General's Medal, because the battalion had been saved thanks to his courage. Then, members of Nozze's unit began to have nightmares; some of them confided in him, elaborating hypotheses as to what had taken place during their abduction.

One night, an inebriated Nozze poured out his heart:

"How have I deserved this medal? I remember the account of the operation, but not the operation as such. It's as if the story had been entirely made up and embedded in my brain."

Nozze's intuition was not brushed aside.

The staff of the Canadian secret service, known for its shrewdness, took charge of the case. Gradually, the truth emerged. The members of the Bologna battalion (as Nozze's unit was called) had undoubtedly been used as guinea pigs in an enemy experiment. Unbeknownst to them, dangerous ideas had been implanted in their brains so that they could be activated remotely after they returned home, thereby transforming them into diabolical weapons.

Research was conducted to elucidate how the enemy had gone about it; it was even necessary to enlist the expertise of American intelligence agents. Following several months of investigation, it was discovered that this conspiracy was to prepare the way for the assassination of an American president in the early 1960s.

Such things are planned well in advance.

*

The mental experiments on the Bologna battalion were carried out by a former student of Pavlov, now head of a team of technicians and neuropsychiatrists.

With great difficulty, the CIA managed to reconstruct the sequence of events. After being abducted, Nozze and his comrades were taken to a research facility where they were subjected to complex procedures designed to repattern their personalities. To prevent the guinea pigs from resisting the experiment, their captors led them to believe, under hypnosis, that they were in a small New England hotel, attending a seminar held by a gardening club on the subject of growing hortensia in limited light conditions. Ordinarily, the colloquial term used is "brainwashing," but in their case, "dry cleaning" or even "expurgation" would be appropriate.

*

Psychological subjection designates all the various attempts to distort an individual's perception of reality through relationships of power, seduction, suggestion, persuasion, or submission. The technique involves the use of an irresistible force that drives one to think or do things against one's will. Hence, when we talk about subjection, we are talking about influence, intrusion, something close to the rape of consciousness and will.

It is no longer I who wants, no longer I who acts; another is within me, another acts through me.

The basic principle, which has been studied since the 1930s, states that a vulnerable individual displays primary avoidance responses that neutralize his capacity for critical thinking and render him manipulable. Moreover, high doses of certain drugs limit the subject's cognitive and discriminating abilities sufficiently for us to condition him as one sees fit.

*

This is the extent of Candice's research so far, supported by documentary evidence and a detailed chronology. I will summarize, synthesize—we each have our strengths. So, here it is. The agents of our own secret service are now developing programs analogous to those undergone in the past by Nozze and his comrades. Drugs are administered to people who unwittingly become guinea pigs for experiments designed to develop techniques of psychological subjection suited to our needs. Conceived by the CIA, these programs are divided into a number of sections and employ people absolutely everywhere.

Experts have dubbed this program, officially named MK-Ultra, Project Bologna, in reference to Giuseppe Nozze's unit. As for Nozze's fate, it can be legitimately described as hard. Convinced by his hypnotizer that he was spending the last years of his life teaching contemporary literature in a university, Nozze, who was actually confined to a convalescence home, was cuckolded a number of times by a swindler who, in an ultimate act of sadism, sent him anonymous letters demanding a payoff if he wished to see his children again, while they were in fact the swindler's offspring.

★

I reread my notes but I'm not sure I've fully understood.

I take my pulse. It's way too high. The CIA, Project Bologna, the use of drugs...the classic themes of the paranoid...I call Candice on the intercom, the door opens, she appears.

"Do you think we're in danger? Who knows if the secret service isn't already giving us low doses of certain drugs in seemingly innocuous preparations?"

"You mean the tap water?"

"Yes, but also the spaghetti sauce in the dining hall. Consider: every day we may be under the influence and possibly manipulated."

"What exactly are you afraid of?"

"Imagine if the people we've just identified decided to track us down, make a clean sweep, eradicate all traces? Imagine if they decided to hurt my children..."

"But, Professor, you don't have children."

"Ah, so I have no children, eh? Well, that's a good one. So who was that marvellous, rambunctious little blond girl I took to the daycare yesterday morning?"

"Yesterday morning at dawn you were found planted

in the snow in front of Ravenscrag, transfixed by the enigma of Bologna."

Hmm, she has a point. I reach into my pocket to take another capsule, but the pillbox is empty. I look for a way to answer Candice as if nothing was the matter, but I'm stuck.

"Are you sure everything's all right, Professor?"

"Really, Candice, just lay off. I've had enough of you pressuring me."

Reddening as though she'd been cut to the quick, Candice looks at me with a blend of anger and empathy and says, "Of course we can each play our different roles — you, the writer pretending not to be naive, me the trained-seal assistant, admiring and sexually inhibited — but when all is said and done, you'll never change. Who do you think you're fooling with this masquerade? People can see the game you're playing; they know that whatever you tell them is meant to hide something... I feel as if I were standing in front of the same little mythomaniac that the police pulled out of the Cinéma Commodore twenty years ago and sent off to Ravenscrag. When will you understand that lying well means telling the truth?"

On that note, Candice turns on her heel and leaves my office, slamming the door just hard enough for my toy soldier to fall on the floor and shatter.

*

Someone wants to harm me, that much is clear.

I take a flask of water out of my jacket and pour a generous amount onto a hand towel, with which I wipe my face to regain my composure. Then I wrap it around my head, à la *Total Recall*, to create interference in the event they try to meddle with my brain.

Now I'm sweating profusely under the towel, but I'm cold at the same time. Something is out of kilter.

I stand up and step toward my objects: the bust of Poe is intact, as is the photo of the orphanage, until the water from the towel drips onto it.

I leave my office in the hope of finding Candice, of persuading her not to abandon me again. For the first time since we met she's not there. I march down the corridors until I reach her office, open the door. She's nowhere to be seen.

I notice a paper raven perched on her file folders. It's a message. Candice bears me no grudge. I can stop fretting.

LA DOLCE VITA

MANY DAYS HAVE GONE BY, yet it's still winter.

Posted at my apartment window in the prone position, focused and vigilant behind the three-metre-wide window, I peer out. Sometimes I succumb to the impression of being on the other side of the pane now, of having turned into the soldier whose fatal bullet I fear when I'm in my office. I succumb to the impression of being the broken figurine. It's no simple matter to cope without my capsules.

Dead calm. The street is deserted.

Yesterday I filched a hole punch from my daughter's pencil case and perforated one of the slats in the venetian blind.

*

My neighbours rarely show up during my watch, but this doesn't prevent my memory of them from inhabiting the silence where I've secluded myself.

Because I miss the time when I was healthy enough to keep up social relationships, I picture my neighbours asking each other: Have you seen Alain lately? How is it he no longer greets us on his way to the office? Is it true that he's taking medication?

It won't be too long before they come knocking at my door.

Meanwhile, when I feel too isolated, stretched out on the floor, I interrupt my surveillance to freshen up. The sensation of water on my skin brings back, almost in spite of myself, high points of our bygone summers.

I see us, my neighbours and me, sitting on the lawn at dusk with the children.

We enumerate our past ailments (Pierre-Louis the pharmacist and his abscessed tooth that evolved into fatal angina; Lilli coming down with hives just when she was opening her notary office); we mention our ethnic origins (Sylvie is Belgian!); we own up to our beliefs (Martin says of Loïc that he has a "old soul") or to our bouts of rage (Carl, incensed by a dog's barking, made it drink solvent); we share our shopping tips (now where did I find that bubble machine for Victor's birthday? At the special

effects shop on boulevard Crémazie, of course!); we spec-
ulate about the future of the cultural industry (Adèle has
just sold a canvas to a wealthy collector in Miami); we
recite our favourite poems (Christine touches us every
time with these words: "I will not be cured of my youth
/ let us go live where life is / or die at least in the sun").

There is a tacit rule in modern literature: you must
vilify Alfred de Musset. Personally, I'm incapable of doing
so for a host of reasons related to his life and work, from
his hatred of the Counter-Revolution to his irreverence
toward Victor Hugo, not to mention his interest, as a true
dandy, in alcohol, gambling, and women.

Do you remember the opening of *The Confession of
a Child of the Century*? No?

Go splash some water on your face, because there's
nothing more beautiful.

*

To write the story of your life, you must first have had
one. Hence, the story that I write is not my own, because
I do not exist.

Just as an injured man with gangrene goes to the
operating theatre to have the rotten limb removed and
the doctor who performs the amputation wraps the sev-
ered limb in a white cloth and sends it circulating from
hand to hand for the medical students to examine, so,

too, when a certain period of a man's existence has been gangrened by disease, he may cut off that portion of himself, detach it from the rest of his life, and send it circulating in the public space, for people to handle it and gauge its desperateness.

Accordingly, I set down what has happened to me since my appointment at McGill. But even if no one takes any notice at all, I shall at least have derived some benefit from my own words: the satisfaction of knowing that I cured myself. Like the fox caught in a snare, I did it by chewing off my trapped foot.

*

Ever since I swallowed the first of the capsules prescribed by Dr. Cameron, my memories surface more readily when I'm in contact with water. I have no idea why, but it works. Look: a light rain wets my hair and already the past has come back.

I have on a cotton jacket with polka dots. I usually wear Italian designer-label suits—the way others wear masks. Sitting on a scorching sidewalk, inside a memory, I watch myself watching the bustling street under a blazing sun. I'm in my mid-twenties; the birth of the Republic of Vietnam has been proclaimed and Eisenhower has sent his first advisers.

I have to stop reading the newspapers.

From one Angelus to the next, I loiter in front of the house — the weather is too fine to write — and I spend the day loafing around, drinking elderberry juice in an insulated plastic cup. As everyone knows, I'm forbidden from drinking alcohol, so I compensate with rare beverages and pharmaceuticals. The children playing hockey in front of the neighbour's house pause and gather around me because they're curious about the figure of the athlete reproduced on the glass that the gas station was giving away with every fill-up. I can't tell if it's Tom Foley, the Montreal Expos shortstop, or a competitor at the Seoul or Albertville Games who will be victorious before failing his drug tests.

One neighbour, a four-year-old blond girl named Émilie, blurts out a peculiar statement: "Your cup comes from the future!"

I don't deny it.

*

Among my yet to be elucidated obsessions are two phenomena related to the consumption of cold drinks: 1) Why is it enjoyable to drink a cold liquid in a plastic cup? 2) Why does the same liquid consumed in a porcelain cup taste different?

Despite all the ablutions I perform so I can linger in the past, my foot is liable to cramp and force me to apprehend my situation once again: the isolation, the blind, the punched out hole.

Fully aware of my hazardous position but less, perhaps, of the factors that plunged me into it, I feel overwhelmed with distress, especially because I have no more capsules to fend off such attacks.

Am I the victim of remotely masterminded manipulations?

Am I falling into the trap of Project Bologna?

Am I Candice's automaton?

No. No. No.

Or maybe yes. In any case, I regain my composure. I refuse to get caught up in paranoid logic, even though my acquaintance with the *Diagnostic and Statistical Manual of Mental Disorders* from a very early age has provided me with a solid grounding in psychology.

A hot bath would calm me down.

*

Come in, I'm underwater. I'll describe out loud the memories that come to me; you should have no trouble understanding me, despite the bubbles.

One rainy day, I visit the Archives Department of the Royal Victoria Hospital on the McGill campus, the very place where, when I was born, a Jewish obstetrician mistakenly circumcised me.

Sitting at a table in a dark corner of what looks like a library, I consult microfilms on the subject of Nab with the diligence of Julia Roberts in *The Pelican Brief*. Who is Nab? My uncle. There, you're following now.

Before residing as a patient there, Nab had worked at Ravenscrag. His invention of a lamp to treat melancholia sparked a great deal of enthusiasm in his community, until the new director decided to replace luminotherapy with another approach, one centred on aquatic immersion. After his dismissal, according to the documents I'm consulting, Nab suffered from severe depression, and he was committed on the recommendation of the new director.

*

I lift my head out of the water when I realize that the coincidence is no coincidence; it was Dr. Cameron who fired Nab and then had him confined. Strange, all the same. You'll tell me there was no need to take a bath to grasp this, that it was easy, that the whole thing was arranged. I'll tell you you're paranoid.

The book you're holding in your hands — the urge to write it came to me twenty years ago, before the events that I'm describing ever occurred. At the time, I was visiting Ravenscrag three times a week to meet with a therapist during her shifts in the psychiatric emergency ward.

What I most recall of this period is the security proto-col to enter that section of the hospital, the metal detec-tors, the guards eyeing me with suspicion when I went to tell them I wasn't insane.

I had been directed to this establishment because Nab was a doctor there. It was always him that my mother called when I had a cold or threw myself down on the floor in a feigned fit of convulsions.

My mother had always been very proud of her younger brother. Every time he appeared on television, I had to stop watching my Japanese cartoons and change the channel.

Nab invented two devices that made his reputation: an electroluminescent diode lamp reputed to heal sea-sonal depression and a helmet with a built-in monitor that reproduced the patients' hallucinations so that the curious might visualize the nature of our nightmares.

My uncle was the first to prescribe me tranquilizers during my difficult adolescent years, in particular, midaz-olam, of which, as I was completing *Matamore no 29* my previous novel, I learned to appreciate the anterograde amnesiac effects. My uncle was the first, but he would not be the last. You find your fun wherever you can. The same holds true for writing.

★

At this particular point in our investigation, I must go back to see Dr. Cameron to have my prescription renewed but, more importantly, to understand what happened to Nab. I would do anything to rid my mind of the image of my uncle's corpse lying in his bed, mouth and eyes half-open, but I feel it will haunt me for a long time.

Before heading out to Ravenscrag, I must take some preventive measures so as not to arouse the suspicions of the watchman Diop.

What I see in the mirror is very bad. I look dead, and the dead are suspect. The solution? In the bathroom there's some leftover makeup that belonged to the Huguenot woman; I hunt through the jars for the darkest foundation and slather my cheeks with it. It's just as bad—no, worse; now I look Moorish. We need to try a different tack.

I wash my face and remember her telling me, when she left her jars, eye shadow, and bottles of perfume in my medicine cabinet, that the Greeks used the same word for "medicine" and "poison." Knowing the double meaning of *pharmakon* helped her to recall that, even if we've been badly hurt, we must sometimes continue to suffer a little to find the right cure.

*

My involvement with the Swiss fashion model began a few years ago while I was studying literature in Europe. It's water under the bridge now, and I act as if the woman no longer exists, yet there are times when I see her again leaning on the handrail, holding a Bellini (white peach purée, Prosecco, a few drops of maraschino cherry juice — they say it's delicious). It was spring then, we were vacationing on the Amalfi Coast, and she spent her days in a bikini. There are moments when I can again see disjointed images of her, a slender hand resting on the guardrail, the bone structure of her foot, her perfect earlobe.

Like most models, she ate sparingly, in order to stay tall and thin. It was probably their interest in this duality that prompted the organizers of the Zurich Motor Show to assign her to the section with the big American cars. That's where we first met. I had decided to attend the show to gather material and to keep Édouard abreast of the latest developments in automotive technology. Some visionaries were predicting that one day car doors would be locked at a distance with a remote control that could also activate the horn. But keep in mind that it's been at least thirty years since they started anticipating the day when we would eat nothing but pills. I'm still waiting.

I approached her by pointing out how unusual it was

to see a model hiding in a car to read a book. I had opened the door to examine the interior and found her inside, engrossed in a paperback edition of Edgar Poe.

I remember that from the moment we began our conversation she was surprised by my accent; she had no idea that French was spoken in Canada. She then told me of her wish to take up residence there in the near future.

I had sat down beside her, in the passenger seat. Funny, we didn't yet know each other and already she was in the driver's seat. We stayed in the car talking for hours. I have a very clear memory of our discussion about, in her words, my noticeable tendency to want to aestheticize each of my gestures. She even gave me a warning—since forgotten—as if she was aware of the risk I was running.

"Be careful. You start by studying literature, you visit motor shows to learn about the latest technological trends for your cousin, and then before too long you find yourself in the middle of a conspiracy where people want to harm you, photographs speak to you, and you're swallowing capsules one after the other."

I held back from telling her she was the love of my life. The Huguenot and I would be together for a while.

*

Life in modern households being what it is, certain irritants arose as soon as I let the Huguenot into my private realm. For instance, whenever I made for the bathroom, right after we had copulated, she was in the habit of telling me, "You don't take your bath like everyone else."

"What do you mean?"

"You don't take your bath to wash."

"It all depends on what you mean by 'wash.'"

That statement became a kind of motto for me. I was unique; I didn't wash like others. Once she got over the annoyance, the Huguenot would smile at me mischievously, pretending not to know that immersing myself in iodine to soak my wounds was the only way for me to stop the bleeding.

I could go on at length about my life with the Huguenot, but you're reading a science fiction novel, not a love story. And if the novel is to move forward, I have no choice but to return to Ravenscrag to meet Dr. Cameron again. I need capsules, I need to understand.

I decide to leave my apartment. I pull on my coat. Wait a minute—I need to get something in the garage.

★

It's strange to go out. The noise outside interrupts the sentences taking shape in my head. Fortunately, I was careful to bring the proper equipment. To keep the roar of the city at bay, I'm wearing the ear protectors that Édouard puts on when his work generates extreme decibel levels.

With the protectors, I have total concentration, despite the din from the scores of construction sites. For the past ten years, the whole downtown area has been filled with the spectacle of skyscrapers going up. I walk in the midst of the feverish activity, but the ear protectors muffle every sound.

★

I climb up the small hill. In the distance, the sculpted raven of Ravenscrag juts out over Diop, the watchman stationed at the entrance to the building.

"So here you are, Professor. I was beginning to worry. Are you finally going to let yourself be persuaded to take advantage of our facilities, to take care of yourself a little, to treat whatever ails you?"

"Hamadou, my friend, I'm glad to see you again. I would like to meet with Dr. Cameron, it's important. Do you think you could take me to him?"

"I'm amused to hear you call me Hamadou."

"Excuse me?"

"You can call me that if you like, but I have to confess it is not my real name."

"I don't understand, Hamadou!"

"And yet it is absolutely true. Racine, my surname, would have sufficed, but alongside the first name that my mother gave me ... I was always the laughingstock of educated people! Two names of fabulous writers — a heavy burden for a child to bear. No wonder I was so unruly all through school and always clashing with authority ... I realized that in life one should not try to understand, and I let myself be guided by curiosity, open-mindedness. Ever since then, I reject all certitudes, I allow events the possibility of filling in the mental territories that I invent as I go along. You know, it's interesting to hit a wall. I would not go so far as to say that I enjoy suffering, but to explore certain avenues one must go through adversity. These things became clear to me when I was a geological dating technician, not too far from here, actually. I operated highly sophisticated instruments, using oxygen-18 and carbon-14 to date works of the Italian Renaissance, large frescoes in particular, like those found in the refectory of my orphanage. One day, my bosses sent me to Ravenscrag to assess the age of the stone where the enigma of Bologna is inscribed, on the other side of the building, the inscription that you spent a whole night contemplating a few weeks ago. Professor, are you sure you are all right?"

My concentration now is such that, even if I don't hear, I understand. The problem is that Diop isn't helping me, speaking like this without making a sound, though, granted, with lots of gesticulations, so that in the end I'm like you: I don't understand what I understand.

*

Early in the sixteenth century, a cobbler from Bologna discovered a heavy metal that emits light when heated. His find created a sensation, and he became the darling of erudite salons and cabinets of curiosity, to such an extent that the tombstones of notables of the region began to be crafted in that material. The most famous of these mortuary monuments remains the stone whose inscription is an enigma that has obsessed aficionados for four centuries but has never been solved.

In 1548, in Venice, Mario Michelangelo published a work of four hundred pages dealing with the enigma. For his part, Count Malvasia, in *Aelia Laelia Crispis non nata resurgens, in expositione legali*, proposes forty-three solutions, including rain, the soul, a child pledged in marriage who, however, dies before being born, an oak, a female *numen* regarded as the source of the fountain, a vase, a mother, the source of life.

In *Mysterium Coniunctionis*, Carl Jung devotes a long chapter to this matter, while Gérard de Nerval refers to the enigma in two of his texts.

Known also as *Aelia Laelia Crispis*, the enigma of Bologna prompted many comments, each of which in its own way reveals the working of the collective unconscious.

Personally, I have no great problem with the enigmatic nature of everything, so long as it doesn't provoke undue angst. If it does, don't worry—I deal with it.

But if you can't deal with it, what do you do then?

*

Aelia Laelia Crispis, neither man, nor woman, nor hermaphrodite, nor girl, nor boy, nor crone, nor chaste, nor prostitute, but all these.

Carried off neither by hunger, nor by sword, nor by poison, but by all these.

Her resting place is neither in heaven, nor in earth, nor in water, but everywhere.

Lucius Agatho Priscius, neither husband, nor lover, nor kinsman, neither mourning, nor rejoicing, nor weeping, raised up for her neither mound, nor pyramid, nor tomb, but all of these.

He knows and does not know what he raised up to whom.

Here is a tomb that holds no body.
Here is a body that no tomb contains.
But a body and a tomb that are one and the same.

★

After a few minutes of trying to read Diop's lips, just when I'm beginning to wonder if I'm suffering from spontaneous deafness, I realize that I'm wearing Édouard's ear protectors. I promptly remove them, hoping that Diop hasn't noticed my absentmindedness.

"What were you saying, Diop, my friend?"

"I was telling you that my work on the strange stone coincided with a kind of call, as though an interior voice was inviting me to undertake a quest to comprehend the foundational structures of the world. Studying the stone made me want to destroy those structures in order to better rebuild them thereafter. One thing led to another, and I eventually turned to architecture."

It's much nicer to have one's hearing back. Trouble is, I know nothing about architecture. I'll set him off on his specialty; it works every time. "Oh, I'm mad about architecture, a subject I'm quite familiar with. Do you design houses?"

"Actually, I attended an experimental school, in Vico Morcote, Switzerland, and earned my living as an apprentice winemaker, though I spent most of my time servicing the vineyard owner's daughter; he no doubt damned me less for deflowering his youngest than for planting his vine shoots upside-down. When I grew tired of my little erotic games, I would drive to La Chaux-de-Fonds, a city built from scratch by Le Corbusier, and get my dose of modernism."

"We might have met each other during one of your trips to that region. I myself visited Emilia-Romagna several times. I have a friend there, a sort of semiologist Casanova."

"We surely must have met. I looked very different then. My skin colour has faded over time. At the time, I attended a school built in the middle of a vast industrial lot. I had expected the facilities to be new, with furniture at the cutting edge of ergonomics. Imagine my surprise at finding myself in a large, completely empty concrete room with neither tables nor chairs. The instructor called his teaching method 'basic training.' When the students began to complain about their aching legs and asked for desks, he said, 'If you want tables and chairs, the materials are outside, and here is your budget for tools. You have carte blanche. Experiment, become what you are, be that makers of tables and chairs.' An original like you may have appreciated that sort of challenge; as for me, I froze."

"Hold on, I'm far from being original. In fact, I go around in circles. Here's proof: I was born in the Royal

Victoria Hospital, just two hundred paces from here, was accidentally circumcised, grew up in the north of the city before I was gambled away by my mother, ran away and was finally confined to a Catholic orphanage."

When Diop hears the last two words, "Catholic orphanage," his eyes react in a peculiar way, not a wink but rather a sort of eyebrow movement. Apparently something is bothering him. I play the innocent.

"Hamadou, I find your academic background fascinating, but I'm here because I must see Dr. Cameron as soon as possible."

"Very well. Unfortunately, you will not be able to meet him. The security procedures have been tightened again since last night."

"And why is that?"

"Someone managed to infiltrate our computer and obtain information on the current experiments. Needless to say, Dr. Cameron is beside himself and has refused to see anyone since. Even his own daughter."

*

I insist for fifteen minutes, itemizing my ailments and symptoms until Diop gives in and finally consents to let me into Ravenscrag. We pass under the stone raven. The floors and corridors multiply below street level, taking us deeper and deeper. I try to stay focused, despite the cries issuing from some of the rooms. Clearly, we're not heading toward the psychiatrist's office.

"I hope you did not assume it would be so easy to gain access to Dr. Cameron... I have explained that when the boss says something, you listen and you stay quiet. That said, a dip in our swimming pool would do you a world of good."

"I'm quite willing to swim a couple of laps if you agree to urge your boss to consider my request."

"Very well. In any event, we first must see Miss Cameron because a specific procedure has just been introduced for new bathers: some of them must put on a cognitive bathing cap before entering the water. I am telling you this although I have no idea what the bathing cap, known here as COBACA, actually does, for the simple reason that no visitor has ever had to wear one until now. This is no doubt a formality. In two short minutes we will receive the authorization and you will be ready to dive in."

*

Diop comes back fifteen minutes later holding a nylon cloth the size of a trivet with various wires and electrodes protruding.

"Miss Cameron expressed a good deal of interest in your case and has carried out a whole series of analyses.

She even succeeded in convincing her father to personally adjust the settings on your cognitive bathing cap. Everything is perfectly ready for your swim."

We set out once again down the corridors of Ravenscrag, guided by the smell of chlorine. Diop, visibly excited, deactivates the alarm system connected to the magnetic entrance; he is about to show me his favourite part of the mansion.

"Welcome to our rest and revitalization zone. You are not obliged to speak right away. Let the effect do its work."

With these words he opens a heavy metal door with a small window of frosted glass.

*

Quite a shock. The swimming pool is surrounded by huge black marble statues reminiscent of those at the Trevi Fountain but twice the size. At one end of the pool is a representation of a dwarf transported by ravens flying in different directions. The ceiling is a gigantic ogival vault covered with Italian frescoes. At the feet of the marble figures, water pours into a pool that I suddenly long to dive into.

I take a step, but Diop stops me and says in a didactic tone of voice: "Once you are in the water, you will tend to sink. Legend even has it that the pool and its system of conduits are connected to the McTavish reservoir, down the mountain, but you know what legends are worth. Otherwise, you are lucky; there is no one here today. The patients only come in the morning for their immersion, while in the evening bathers come and do as they please. I believe the boss's daughter wanted you to have it all to yourself. She checked the surveillance monitors before authorizing me to bring you here."

I smile, but I wouldn't mind taking my leave of the watchman long enough to slip into my bathing suit. He, however, doesn't budge and keeps such a close eye on me that if I weren't aware of his taste for women I would conclude he was eager to see me in my birthday suit. So I get mentally prepared to stand naked before him, remove my jacket, my shoes, my tie, my shirt, my trousers, and my socks.

Diop is surprised by my tattoos: "Your bodily decorations are impressive."

Quite unexpectedly, he moves closer, grabs my left arm and lifts it up to examine the two stars tattooed on the inside, and then inquires about the meridian that runs down my back from nape to coccyx.

"What is the meaning of the small perpendicular lines that cross the long vertical line?"

"They stand for the deaths in my life. Each time I lose someone dear to me I have a horizontal line tattooed, so that I carry on me the stigmata of the past."

"There is a very recent one; I can tell from the scab."

"Yes, it's in memory of my uncle Nab, who died a few months ago."

Without responding, the watchman looks down to my bathing suit.

"Your swimsuit is unique. I have never seen one like it, ample and variegated. The flower designs conjure up the islands!"

"A friend brought it back from a voyage in the Pacific. May I dive in now?"

"Yes, all you need to do is to put on the COBACA."

I feel the anxiety brought on by a visit to the dentist's.

The watchman gingerly fastens the device to my head using adhesive paper that amplifies the electrical contact. The cap is soon installed, one electrode on my left temple, another on my right temple. Once all the connections have been hooked up, it resembles a shower cap.

I experience a novel sensation: my scalp hurts, as if that part of my body were all at once superfluous. I step slowly toward the swimming pool. Diop signals that I can go in.

*

Because I'm sensitive to the cold, I step into the water following the order of my limbs when I'm in the upright position. The water isn't very cold, but I dread the immersion of my groin. If you have testicles, you will understand what I mean.

Once the pelvic phase is over, I feel lighter. As my head descends toward the surface of the water, memories come rushing back; I'm floating in a pliant, lukewarm matrix adapted to my size. I'm in the right place. All is well.

I dip my head into the water and watch the raven sculptures undulating above the surface and blurring until the darkness of the marble blends with that of the water.

The cap seems to be working without a hitch. My scalp has stopped hurting, but I touch my head and notice that under the nylon cloth my hair is gone; my skull is soft at various points, and my fontanelles have opened up. We're making progress.

*

"Push, Mrs. Safi, push, you're almost there."

The obstetrician is urging my mother on in English. My head is well into her vagina, but — try it yourself — it's easier to enter than to exit. I try to shift my position, pushing my whole skull against the mucus and blood, and my advancing forehead crushes my mother's intestines.

I'm afraid my nose will end up wallowing in feces; what a peculiar way to start out, surrounded by billions of bacteria. To be fair to the medical staff, I've seen in a report that the personnel are thoroughly trained to deal with this kind of situation.

A nurse takes over from the obstetrician and shouts, *"Poussez, madame Safi, allez-y!"*

My mother will find it reassuring to be spoken to in French.

I let myself sink deeper into the swimming pool while extricating myself from my mother. Then I feel a powerful muscular contraction.

All at once, I'm cold, as if I had a skin for the first time.

I pass from one medium to the other; the air becomes my new water. I am born.

The obstetrician congratulates my mother. Seeing that she doesn't understand, the nurse translates into French: "Congratulations, Madame, it's a boy. Don't worry, I've arranged the circumcision, everything's taken care of. If I may be so bold as to share a smidgen of my Hebraic knowledge, just this very morning, the rabbi of a synagogue to which I made a generous donation blessed my house with a Torah handwritten by scribes in Jerusalem. It's a very good sign for the baby. So you were wrong not to want to give birth at the Royal Victoria."

Despite the analgesics and the repairs to the pudendal block, my mother manages to say that her perennial fear of Victorian buildings is beyond her control. The nurse, still acting as interpreter, answers, "Madame, you must abandon these superstitions."

*

I continue to swim, I continue to sink, yet I have the impression of rising. Is it possible that I'm already swimming toward the surface?

I consider resisting, but another period of my past sweeps me along.

*

For several days, I've been shut inside the white cube at the back of our apartment at the Topaze in Cartierville. According to my mother, this is the safest place for me, medically speaking. Lacking windows, the room prevents drafts and eliminates any possibility of my being in contact with harmful chemical sprays. I spent part of my childhood in this sealed room. That may seem appalling. It is.

My mother comes to see me often and strictly monitors my ingesta and excreta as well as my transpiration. As far back as I can recall, she speaks to me in medical terms. She frequently cites *Mille secrets, mille dangers*, a medical reference book for the layperson, which serves as both her Bible and handbook for fighting diseases.

Guided by it, my mother has devised a diet based on one fundamental law: avoid mixtures at all costs.

The rules of the diet are complex. Let me give you an example. Because they are bovine in origin, milk products must never be eaten with tomato dishes, as the acidity of the latter alters the cellular structure of milk, which may sour as a result. The so-called "pink sauce" argument is often invoked to challenge the validity of that hypothesis. To anyone unfamiliar with the biochemical antagonisms of her milk/tomato theory, my mother's response may appear sibylline: There is no evidence that this type of molecularly altered sauce did not cause the poisoning of forty-six young French students in Salerno, south of Naples, in 1937, just before the introduction of Mussolini's racist policy.

You have nightmares after eating *tartiflette*? It's the same principle.

*

Eggs, too, must be served with caution.

For two hours before and after eggs are ingested, eating fish is forbidden. My mother has noticed that this combination induces sweating. And transpiration is prohibited at all times, day or night, January or June. Every hour, my mother makes sure that I'm not perspiring, that my second-generation immigrant's undershirt isn't damp.

In her system, nothing is worse than perspiration. If there happens to be a draft, if I catch cold, the consequences are catastrophic. For days, my mother rubs me down very hard; curiously, it's when she subjects me to this treatment that I have the worst stomach aches, and I start bleeding again.

When my condition worsens, she rails at fate, wonders what she did to the Good Lord to deserve a child so prone to illness, so fragile, her life a sacrifice even though she has given me everything.

*

How long have I been underwater?

Where is my oxygen coming from?

Has my flesh shrivelled?

How can I force myself to the surface again when the past is pulling me down toward the bottom?

Time doesn't matter anymore, I am a man-fish, I sway amid the currents.

*

Because I'm a child requiring special care and constant monitoring, and because a mixture or perspiration can occur so abruptly, my mother can't work. She has no choice but to sacrifice everything for me. So, although

I'm only eight or nine years old, I do my best to bring home some money. Every evening, on my way back from school, I go from door to door selling ornamental soaps. My route through the streets of Cartierville sometimes leads me to the Institut Albert-Prévost, where I come across Mr. Aquin, the commander of the Special Organization, sitting by the rivière des Prairies and often busy writing in his notebook. Some days, when sales are meagre, I have to cross the Lachapelle bridge to L'Abord-à-Plouffe, where, on learning that my mother is Lebanese and that I'm working to provide for both of us, the residents respond generously.

Selling soap, however, isn't enough to pay for rent and food, so my mother finds other ways of earning money, including gambling. She repeats that, since she doesn't drink, smoke, or go out with men, this little vice of hers shouldn't cause us any problems.

Thirty years on, immersed in water with no resources other than a technologically sophisticated bathing cap, my paranoia, and a cockamamie story, I don't think I'm in a position to pass judgement on my mother.

*

All things considered, my mother's vice does cause us problems. To offset her losses and increase her income — the soaps aren't enough — she bets more and more often

on horses and buys my silence by ignoring her own principles and taking me to the giant orange next to the
racetrack. Hermas Gibeau, creator of the Orange Julep,
uses eggs in his juice, a blend proscribed by the table of
mixtures.

For reasons unknown to me even now, my mother
decides that her fortune will come through a purebred
Arabian called Smooth Muscle. This horse will make us
wealthy, give us the wherewithal to buy a concession in
Cochinchina, and one day finance the purchase of my
Italian suits.

Obviously, nothing goes as planned. The debts keep
piling up despite the schemes and calculations that my
mother works out using her rudimentary accounting
skills. To navigate these dire straits, she notes her hare-
brained computations on little scraps of paper. She says
she can make sense of these scrawls. I know that she
can't. Her argument stays unchanged: I don't drink, I
don't smoke, I don't have a boyfriend, and it's not some
measly little vice that's going to ruin our lives.

The months go by and the pressure mounts. Our situation quickly becomes intolerable. Little by little we sell
off most of our possessions—the Zenith television set,
the Royal Albert dinnerware, the rosewood credenza,
the transistor radio, the rolls of cellophane wrap, and
the remaining soaps—leaving the sapphires and emer-
alds until the very last moment. Then my mother starts

to borrow money from the so-called big shots who hang around the Topaze, the shameless embezzlers of the neighbourhood's old ladies. Their cash helps us for a time, in particular to pay for the funeral of Teta Aïda, my grandmother.

Very soon, however, there are people knocking at the door to collect the capital and interest on the loans. At first, I don't get involved in the negotiations; from the windowless room, I listen to the tense, sometimes heated conversations between my mother and her creditors.

Things get complicated the day my mother sends me to answer the door while she takes her turn hiding in the white cube where she has forced me to live. So the big shots lay into me instead.

Lozeau and Kid Godin are the ones who frighten me most. I can't say if it's the leather jacket and stained boots of the former or the alcohol-tainted breath and scarred face of the latter. Twice they wreck our living room, bellowing like animals, plug the sinks with dishtowels to make them overflow, help themselves to the contents of the fridge, smash our alabaster replicas of the Giza pyramids on the floor. Today, as if they're fed up with this futile waste of energy, they give me an ultimatum.

Whenever I'm threatened, I resist—I can't help it. I let these so-called big shots know that no one has ever seen a well-digger draw water from a stone, that they won't get anything from us, that they shouldn't have loaned money to my mother, that she's responsible, that they can kill her if they feel like it, but that, as for me, I've had it with this situation, and I have to go study for my exams.

Lozeau's answer echoes inside the COBACA: "Farah, even if you go to school for the rest of your life, you'll always be a fucking import, a Cartierville loser, and, anyway, if you don't pay up it won't be your mother that gets killed, but you."

★

One night, my mother declares that if we want to keep the apartment she has to win big, no matter if the risk we take is just as big. When the neighbours start showing up at our house one by one or in small groups, I realize that our apartment is about to be transformed, for an evening, into a clandestine casino.

Once the dice table has been set up, my mother asks me to sit in an armchair in the middle of the room. Now I'm bombarded by the greedy gazes of our neighbours, corpulent Armenian ladies wearing costume jewellery and smelling of sweat. They grin at me with mouthfuls of loose teeth, their eyes filled with craving and lust.

My mother, who knows that I know, steps closer and whispers in my ear, "Don't worry, they'll never have enough money to bet on you."

In the end, the evening is fairly successful. My mother wins, she's happy, tells me she loves me, and I end up thinking that the casino may have been a good idea after all. But at the stroke of midnight the door opens and in walks a very rich guest wearing, like all good Lebanese parvenus, genuine gold jewellery. Her escorts are Lozeau and Kid Godin. She signals to my mother that she would like to have a closer look at me. Her flunkies bring me to her. Without the slightest hesitation, she takes down my pants and fingers my testicles. Turning to my mother as I pull my pants back up, she says, "I've always dreamt of possessing a little Jew like him."

*

An electric discharge inside the cap is creating interference. Suddenly, I have the impression of rising to the surface, my ears unblock, and I see a halo of light that slowly dilates.

It's time for me to get out of the water.

*

The wealthy, gold-bedecked Lebanese woman bets methodically until the roll of the dice finally lets her walk away with me.

It's quite something, believe me, to see your mother's

face when she's lost her entire winnings for the night and her son at the same time.

Kid Godin steps toward me to hand me over to my new owner, but Lozeau cuts in and says to us, "Don't start moaning that we've stolen your baby, Madame Safi. You lost him yourself. And you, Farah, you'll see that the boss will take care of you. She won't gamble you away."

This statement triggers an explosion in my brain, and I start to run, taking off without even putting on my boots.

Once out the door of the Topaze, I dash down the dark streets of Cartierville to boulevard Gouin, passing in front of the Institut Albert-Prévost along the way. I don't know if the big shots are following me. I look straight ahead, wonder where to go, run across boulevard Laurentien and past the big sign of the Commodore. Barely slowing down, I rush into the theatre.

I'm aware that dimly lit rooms are the worst places to hide out, but put yourself in my situation: I'm now motherless, and my feet are frozen and bloody.

*

Let's be clear: At the Topaze, the hub of the Lebanese ghetto where I grew up, the Lozeaus and Godins are scarce. Knowing this, should I have christened my big shots Abdel, Shafik, or Mr. Youssef and given them a coveted position in the hierarchy of the street gangs that clone ATM cards at the filling station?

No. I'm not a sociologist. Confusion is my method.

Supplementary question: Before being converted into a video club, did the Commodore even once present Jean-Claude Lauzon's *Léolo*, my source for Lozeau and Godin?

No, but at times I imagine myself sitting in that room, in the darkness, alongside Édouard, watching looped scenes from the films of that great director. An old man in a wheelchair with a rifle shoots an elephant in a zoo; Italy bursts out of a closet in the Mile-End district.

A Cessna crashes in a spruce forest on the edge of a crater in New Quebec.

*

My feet gradually warm up. I've been ensconced in the back row for ten minutes or so, watching a newsreel in which Hitler's troops are shown marching on Poland, when the police burst into the theatre to grab me.

They interrogate me in a room adjacent to the projection booth.

To avoid accusing my mother, I make up an absurd story, telling them that I come from the future and have painlessly materialized in this movie theatre, that they shouldn't worry, it's fabulous where I come from, the inhabitants live on a diet of pills, everyone has a movie theatre in their home, and time travel is commonplace.

They don't seem to attach much importance to my story and apparently have no intention of relaying it to the FBI. Before dawn, the bureaucratic authorities order that I be transferred to the Augustin Roscelli Catholic Orphanage. Some Italian nuns give me a generous welcome and pair me up with Montaigne Racine, a Haitian who sneezes the first time I say hello. I'm relieved, less to have found a new friend than to have slipped through the bejewelled claws of a Lebanese nabob.

*

I'm nearing the surface of the water but am unable to reach it, as if something is slowing me down. I tear off the cognitive cap and immediately begin to suffocate, but with a few vigorous strokes I finally come up. I'm astonished to realize that I'm now swimming in a large, dome-covered lake. When I get to the shore, I look around for the way out — this is far from simple — among the narrow concrete corridors that run along massive tanks many storeys high. Shivering, I grope my way along in the dark for a few minutes and soon find an exit. I open it, though I'm less than thrilled at the thought of going out wet, bare-chested, in Bermudas. Once outside, there's no mistaking my whereabouts. I'm standing across from my building, on the other side of avenue McGregor, by the McTavish reservoir.

I must have been transported here through a network of pipes.

I need to speak with Candice. Assuming that she's in her office as usual.

I cross the street, barefoot in the snow.

*

I march quickly down the corridors of the McGill Arts Building, taking care not to slip. I'm hurrying because I'm eager to see my assistant again. She'll appreciate my report; it's good material.

When I arrive at her office — surprise! Sitting in Candice's chair, legs crossed, Salomé greets me with a smile of assurance mixed with relief. Just as she did at the Place Ville Marie inauguration, she takes the initiative in the conversation. "Something you said on the evening we met stayed with me for a long time: a kiss could kill if beauty is not death... Like you, I'm very fond of Mallarmé."

"You came here in the middle of the night to discuss literature?"

"I was curious in particular about where your latest peregrinations have taken you. Since we met, I've reread the Gospels. Do you know which is my favourite scene?"

"Pray tell."

"Jesus asks a possessed man his name, to which the latter answers, 'Legion, for we are many.' It made me think of you, because your books are important to me. So, how is your novel coming along? I recently read in a periodical that your book will deal with the connections between McGill and the CIA. Is that true?"

"Listen, Salomé, I'll be frank with you. You're a vivacious, clever young woman, but I don't really appreciate finding you in my assistant's office as if nothing was wrong. Your being here tonight suggests that you're unbalanced."

*

"The virtues of balance are overrated. Eco told me that what you are after is intensity. You are ill, Professor; come closer, and I will be your cure."

"It's touching that you should be concerned about my health. I'd forgotten that you were a determined woman."

"Have you read the book I gave you before you left so abruptly the night of the inauguration? Memories can be implanted in the brain; the necessary technology exists."

"That's very interesting, but tell me, I was hoping to see my assistant. As this is her office..."

"You're referring to that unpleasant, frigid Swiss

woman who is here twenty-four hours a day?"

"Candice must find you vulgar, and I can see why."

"Don't be angry. Only, tell me where you've been in those smart flowered Bermudas."

"That's none of your business."

"True, you're free to go swimming in the middle of the night if you so wish."

"Has anyone asked for your permission?"

"I thought the swimming pool was located at *the top* of the mountain, behind the psychiatric hospital, but here you are down *below*, in your bathing trunks, drenched to the bone."

"I'm tired, and you won't get a word out of me."

"You are definitely bad company tonight, Professor. I thought there was a bond between us. No matter. As I did at our first meeting, I would like to present you with a gift that will give you food for thought. And the next time we see each other, I will give you the same treatment that Christ gave the Adversary: I will draw you out of your body."

At this, Salomé deposits a flat, square box on the table, gets up from Candice's armchair, and brushes past me as she leaves the room.

*

Home, at last. The taxi driver who brought me back looked surprised to see a bare-chested man in Bermudas in the middle of winter, but he asked no questions.

I place the peculiar gift from Salomé in front of me on the kitchen table. It's circular, mirrored on one side, black on the other, and printed on it, in vaguely Chinese script, are the words WU-TANG CLAN, ENTER THE WU-TANG (36 CHAMBERS). A strange wall decoration. Candice will find me a frame.

I'll catch my death of cold, but even though I'm frozen to the bone I don't feel up to taking a bath. I won't look at the clock. I don't want to find out that the night is almost gone. It's out of the question to do anything at all without at least eight solid hours of sleep, especially since I'm no longer protected by my capsules and Dr. Cameron appears to be inaccessible now.

For the moment, the best thing I can do is to sink comfortably into my armchair and let sleep overtake me, in the same way that people tranquilize themselves with chemical substances.

I switch on the TV. Maybe my Japanese science fiction series is on tonight.

*

No such luck: there's an Italian film playing.

A helicopter is carrying a statue of Jesus to St. Peter's Basilica, followed by another helicopter, in which the hero, Marcello, convinces the pilot to detour over a large terrace where two superb, bikini-clad girls are sunbathing.

I know them, the two girls.

The first is an identical copy of Candice: blond, willowy, honest. The second reminds me of Salomé, with her come-hither look, her dark hair, and her makeup, which is more sophisticated than a Bernini sculpture. As for me, I obviously identify with Marcello, a former press photographer, more ambitious than his friend Paparazzo since he dreams of becoming a writer.

We're in Rome, on the runway of an airport, the weather is absolutely splendid, and everyone is looking at Sylvia, a Hollywood star, who, on alighting from the airplane, is presented with a pizza.

Sylvia, the most beautiful woman in all creation. In her, the body and the image of the body are sundered.

You can reread that. I'm not sure what I'm trying to say; I only know that I can look at pictures of Anita Ekberg in the Trevi Fountain with the same veneration that I felt when, as a little boy, I looked at pictures of women in underwear in the Sears catalogue.

*

Does neoliberalism have a future? A journalist asks Sylvia this question as she disembarks from the airplane.

The character played by Ekberg is a creature of the surface. This becomes clear when she enjoys herself in a club located amid Roman ruins, surrounded by men who lust after her, as she dances to rock and roll music or tells me, after picking up a lost kitten, "It needs milk, *bello*. Go find some!"

I go.

The sisters at the Catholic orphanage knew full well: Italy is fertile ground for miracles. Even though the film is not reality, two children witness the apparition of the Virgin in a vacant lot, while sheep are blocking traffic on a highway.

The night and the silence weigh on me. I watch TV and, through the power of thought, I attempt to meet up with Marcello on the beach, and to be served a refreshing drink by Émilie, my daughter.

We could go out, Marcello and I, until four in the morning, eat pasta and flirt with the waitresses in the middle of the night, but in the film my evenings are spent mainly in villas, old castles where, among the jaded heirs to aristocratic fortunes, I try to flush out ghosts, old friends, lost loves.

I love this character life, this sweet life, without

psychology, this life of the surface. I would like for it to end with a woman's monologue or a scene of mental orgy, but I know in advance that I'll end up standing before a huge sea creature lying inert on the beach, and after frittering the night away, I'll hear Émilie, my child, my daughter, separated from me by a brook, telling me, "I'm here to save you." Too caught up in transcribing what I see on the television, I won't hear her and will perish in silence.

★

A faint sound coming from the vestibule interrupts my transcription of the Fellini film. An envelope appears under the door. I hope that Salomé hasn't followed me.

Through the hole in the blind I discern the silhouette of a woman slightly taller than me, her blond hair gathered up in a chignon, her striped dress of mid-thigh length. She walks away at a rapid pace.

I consider putting my trousers back on and following her, but I drop the idea when I notice that on the envelope lying on the vestibule floor are the words, "From Candice."

★

Dear madman,

We have not seen each other since our last argument. You

have probably surmised that I have decided to step back and to stop playing your little game. I hope you are well and that you have gotten a better grip on your anxieties.

As for me, I have of course not stopped working on our project. I continue to make discoveries, but I am somewhat anxious about your reaction.

You remember MK-Ultra, Project Bologna? It turns out the program is not restricted to military institutions; the CIA's tentacles also extend into the academic world. I have identified no fewer than seventy research institutions and a hundred and eighty-five researchers engaged in developing behaviour control methods. That is not all: through a cover called the Institute for Human Ecology Studies, the CIA secretly finances some fifty universities in twenty-one countries.

Can you see where this is going?

I was able to confirm, by accessing his laboratory's computer, that Ewen Cameron, the Allan Memorial's chief psychiatrist, receives funds from the American intelligence agency's front organization. I also have in my possession proof that he administers depatterning treatments to the patients of his clinic. Cameron deprives them of sleep for periods of up to several days, has them take various drugs, and forces them to listen for weeks to recorded messages while strapped down to a special stretcher. His depatterning experiments are based on the hypothesis that by erasing an individual's memory one can completely reprogram him and rid him of any psychotic or criminal traits.

I tried to investigate this further to understand how so many reputed scientists could participate in what is now being called brainwashing. Note that this type of coercive indoctrination designed to re-educate people by reshaping their thoughts is nothing new; one need only recall the exorcisms of individuals possessed by demons and the casting of magic spells, not to mention magnetism and hypnosis. Even your mother's fascination with the evil eye borders on this. But the most terrifying notion concerns the stage prior to reprogramming, which involves actually depatterning the psyches of individuals so as to produce a circular logic and to give them the impression they are ill, that they are not right in the head. Cameron's patients are put through extreme psychiatric shock treatment. While already under the influence of barbiturates and LSD, they are subjected to massive electroshock.

So far so good? Can you deal with this? For my sake, go have a drink of water.

Okay.

I would have preferred to tell you the following in person, but I was afraid you would turn aggressive again and revert to your old habits, the ones you had before therapy.

What I am about to disclose will hurt you: your uncle Nab was on the verge of publicly denouncing Cameron's practices. I have no evidence that he caused Nab's death, but you must admit that it was a strange coincidence. I have not succeeded in getting my hands on information that could incriminate him. Should we talk to Édouard about this?

On perhaps a lighter note, I suppose you have resumed your nights of cruising with the Italian: a vamp has been hanging around your office more and more often. At first, I found her pathetic, but lately she has become a menace, so I am pursuing my research at home. Why not drop in to see me when you feel up to it.

Over,

Your Huguenot

36 CHAMBERS

WHAT'S WORSE, NOT WAKING from a nightmare or dreaming that you're not asleep?

I stare at the ceiling fan—maybe by interpreting its circular movement I can arrive at an answer. Because what's worse, not waking from a nightmare or dreaming that you're not asleep?

I don't know.

Candice says nothing about this in the letter she slipped under my door a few days ago. Still, I reread it compulsively, articulating each word out loud. I carry these words in my head. This morning, too exhausted to get to the toilet, I ended up telling myself, as I urinated into the plant pot next to my bed, that, after all, it may have been me who'd written it. Could I have written it and sent it to myself?

We're going around in circles.

I have to get rid of it, the letter—it's dangerous. I fold and refold the pages into triangles until they begin to take the shape of a raven. I place it on my night table. Well, that's taken care of. To each his juju.

The origami session has revitalized me. Riding a surge of energy possibly born of despair, I slip into my pyjamas. I remember that the documents Candice left on my doorstep two days ago are on the kitchen table. They detail the career of Ewen Cameron, the man I intend to destroy.

As I leave the bedroom, I have second thoughts: if the documents were to make me feel sick, what should I do with them? Origami using a thousand pages held together with a spiral binding—what would that look like? A herd of unicorns?

*

To recapitulate. In 1938, Dr. Ewen Cameron leaves his native Scotland, settles in Albany, publishes prolifically.

When McGill hires him in September 1943, the aim is not solely to entrust him with the mandate of directing Royal Victoria's Department of Psychiatry; he is also called upon to transform Ravenscrag into a progressive, ultra-modern psychiatric hospital bearing the name Allan Memorial Institute.

Cameron's reputation for integrity is such that he is invited to the Nuremberg trial to provide an assessment of Nazi Rudolf Hess's mental health. This experience plays a crucial role in his search for the means to heal the diseased part of the human psyche, the part that led people to commit certain well-known acts during the Second World War.

When it launches Project Bologna in 1953, the CIA sets about finding academics to carry it out. The CIA recruits Cameron early on and, through a cover organization, makes arrangements to secretly provide long-term funding for his depatterning experiments out of the agency's budget.

Is it the failure to cure the human psyche of its torments that, over time, frustrates Cameron? Who knows? In any event, the facts remain unchanged: the doctor increases the intensity of the treatments administered to his patients — more electroshocks, more drugs, more depatterning messages. Then, in 1964, he retires, settles comfortably in the New York area, where he dies three years later while hiking.

*

For the sake of intellectual honesty, I should qualify my statements about Cameron and stress the fact that he succeeded in turning Montreal into a world-class centre for avant-garde psychiatry. Because, while five thousand mental patients, including the poet Émile Nelligan, were languishing in the Hôpital Saint-Jean-de-Dieu, Cameron was the first psychiatrist to propose treating such patients in external clinics, thereby offering an alternative to institutionalization and social stigmatization.

But intellectual honesty is the least of my concerns.

What matters above all is to wreak revenge on my enemy. And, as Socrates and Sun Tzu said, know thine enemy, know thee thyself, and thou shalt be victorious.

*

In the meantime, my life has gone back to normal, which means that I'm eating cereal while watching TV. Tonight, there's a rerun of a public affairs program. I'm struck by the host's introduction: "Our guest today is a psychiatrist at the Allan Memorial Institute, and he will be talking about a case that goes back to the fifties and was resolved yesterday in Washington. The parties finally arrived at a settlement, and the CIA has agreed to pay damages to Canadians who served as guinea pigs to a Montreal doctor working on behalf of the agency. Dear friends, please give a warm welcome to Dr. Nab Safi."

After allowing a few moments of applause, the woman hosting the show quickly cuts to the chase: "Dr. Safi, the treatments to which Dr. Cameron subjected his patients—what did they consist of?"

"He would administer a series of electroshocks to people who had come to a walk-in clinic to consult him, often for minor problems of anxiety. Cameron believed he could cure them by reprogramming their brains."

"Was this therapy considered acceptable in 1962?"

"It should be recalled that today's drugs did not exist. Treatment was limited to cold showers, hot baths, and electroshocks."

"We're talking about electroshocks forty times stronger than a normal dosage, aren't we?"

"Yes. But the poor reputation of the procedure is due in particular to its being carried out without anaesthetics."

"No one objected?"

"Dr. Cameron had an excellent reputation. He was not a charlatan and he was the head of a well-respected hospital. All this should be seen from the viewpoint of those times. That said, the experiments had major effects on the memory and mental functions of the patients. Cameron effectively deprogrammed them, but the reprogramming stage was a failure."

"I understand. And for the benefit of our viewers, could you give us some particulars as to what patients are being offered today? Previously on our program, you were invited to explain your electroluminescent diode lamp, but are there more radical methods for treating mental health problems?"

"Twenty percent of patients do not respond to medication or the lamp that we have developed. To treat them, we work on the deep regions of the brain, those that produce sadness, negative thoughts, madness. An advanced technique exists whereby a very fine electrode is implanted in the brain through the pores of the scalp."

"That's fabulous, Dr. Safi."

*

I'm clicking away like a maniac on my Jerrold. It's the only sound in the house as I randomly zap through the channels and push back the limits of technology — 10 is on 7, 2 is on 4 — to make sure the dead don't take control of the screen.

I come across *Sauver les meubles*, on Canal Vie, a home decorating series that Candice and I enjoyed in the days of our domesticity.

Today's show is about bathroom remodelling and features an analysis of a layout strategy that made it possible to move the shower north of the bath and to align the bidet, dressing table, and toilet bowl in keeping with the principles of good taste. Following several essentially phatic exchanges, the host asks the guest designer to explain the modus operandi that guided him during the conception of this very bold lavatory.

Here is his response: "I work simultaneously on the

specific and general levels. Here, I've tried to conserve the character and spirit of 1962 while projecting myself into 2012. Or vice versa, I'm not quite sure."

What an idiot.

★

The television has been on for days. I see it without watching, unable to staunch the flow of my thoughts.

I won't turn it off. I need it. For a long time, I've had the impression it's all I have left.

When I was young and ill, imprisoned in a white cube, it was literally my only window on the world. The only thing I could do was to switch on the TV and to vanish into things. Like Emma Bovary, I had my most beautiful experiences in front of the television.

The series *Scoop* affected me so deeply that at the end of the final episode I decided to become a journalist. Just like the character played by Roy Dupuis, I was in love with Stéphanie Gendron, a.k.a. Macha Grenon, unaware at the time that this actress would play an important role in *The Sleep Room*, a series based on the bestselling novel, *Dr. Cameron's Victims*.

*

Around the mid-nineties, shortly after the explosion of the atomic bomb in Hiroshima, on the day after a particularly exciting episode of *Scoop* in which the protagonists foiled a monstrous plot, I confided to Mr. Cho, my French literature teacher, that I intended to study journalism and marry Macha Grenon. He suggested that I try writing and, in so doing, gave me a taste for literature.

At his request, I hatched a short dystopia featuring Allan, an unreliable narrator. He pretended to be shooting a film depicting a decrepit America under the sway of a consortium of covert doctors who cured people by administering intravenous drugs and ingestible capsules.

My protagonist was a Blade Runner, that is, a dealer who supplied the consortium with drugs sold to him cheaply by wholesalers.

Very soon in my story, Allan contracted a virus that opened a hole in time and thus destabilized the chronology: one foot in the past, one foot in the future, and Allan lost in the middle.

As the plot unfolded, the reader, with due diligence, came to understand Allan's true nature: he was a robot endowed with language and free will.

My character's artificiality helped him survive in a riot-ridden Manhattan, where the drugs were fifty times more potent than the midazolam that I began taking in those days; they were, in other words, lethal.

*

Mr. Cho appreciated my piece while appearing unfazed by my plagiarism of William Burroughs's *Blade Runner*; in fact, he was happy to inform me that the American writer had himself plagiarized Alan Nourse's *The Blade Runner*. I wonder if Mr. Cho was aware that, just when Burroughs published his book, a guy was labouring on a screen adaptation of Philip K. Dick's short story, "Do Androids Dream of Electric Sheep?"

The screenwriter had a title problem. Neither *Mechanismo*, nor *Android*, nor *Dangerous Days* was to his liking. For his film adaptation of Dick's story he needed something more powerful. We know how hard it is to christen a work, characters, children — let's not go over that again.

Even though the stories were completely different, the screenwriter decided to adopt Burroughs's and Nourse's title, and Ridley Scott's great dystopia became the third work of fiction in the space of a decade to bear the title *Blade Runner*.

I'd like to be able to discuss all this with my old literature teacher, and also to tell him that I quickly dropped my plans to become a journalist, but a few weeks after our class graduated from high school Mr. Cho hanged himself in the gymnasium. I'd like to know if the ghosts that haunted him, before he did the deed, had any relation to literature.

I wish I were a character in a novel and could travel through time, find Cho at the nadir of his despair, and give him a few of my capsules.

But that's impossible, and you know the reason why: my capsules have run out.

*

In Ridley Scott's version, Blade Runners are no longer on the side of the small-time gangland bosses; now they uphold the established order and support the powers that be. They hunt replicants: humanoid robots that can be identified and distinguished from humans only through complex ocular tests.

The Blade Runner is expected to rid the city of replicants. He must fulfill his mission at all costs, even if this sometimes means embedding a bullet in a robot's head. Whatever method is used in the process, when a Blade Runner eliminates a replicant, he is said to have "retired" him.

*

I saw Scott's film at least five times at the Commodore with Édouard. Each time, my cousin was amazed to see me on the edge of my seat, enthralled to the point of forgetting my anxieties about the dislocated images. That Los Angeles of 2019, built during the early eighties in a Hollywood studio, that bleak, intense, overcrowded, Asian Los Angeles, swallowed me whole. Because, unlike other sci-fi movies, *Blade Runner* is not a story of detectives pursuing androids, but a fable about existential disquiet, about the arbitrary definition of reality, about the question of creation and control.

The following statement, not surprisingly, has been ascribed to the director: "I never think in a linear way. I put everything that matters to me in a bag, I shake it and I watch what happens."

*

After the screening of the film's first cut, the stunned producers of *Blade Runner* confessed to Scott, "Ridley, your film is superb, but we don't understand a thing."

Is it terrible to not understand a thing, if it's beautiful?

The producers' answer: yes, it's terrible.

But can't the emotion felt be just as important as understanding the plot?

No.

The director, who, unlike the writer, rarely enjoys total freedom, agreed to have an inept voice-over foisted on his film, making Harrison Ford sound like a tour guide: *Good evening, I'm Deckard, I don't dream about unicorns, how is it that the leader of the replicants just spared my life when he had me in his sights?*

In addition to the didactic narration, the producers insisted that Scott conclude the film with a less ambiguous ending, one that completely perverted the project. For the final scene, where Deckard and the disturbing replicant flee from the city, fog prevented the film crew from shooting the bucolic landscapes that, in a spirit of crude Manichaeism, were supposed to contrast with the director's decadent and sinister Los Angeles.

Scott consequently suggested borrowing the shots from *The Shining* that Stanley Kubrick had edited out of the opening scene. Kubrick consented, knowing that art, in whatever form, is primarily a matter of collage.

*

But we've strayed from the subject, more specifically my nightmares.

Almost every night since arriving at the orphanage, I dream that I murder a dwarf and then, realizing that I must get rid of the body post-haste, chop it into pieces, stuff them into garbage bags, and deposit the bags all around the city. The horror, for me, doesn't lie in the events concocted by my imagination, but in the nature of the incidents depicted in my nightmare: Did I or did I not commit the acts that I see myself committing there? Each morning, for five minutes, I fixate on this question, until I realize that if I had really committed such a crime, I must surely have left clues, and if I did leave clues, the police would surely arrest me. This reasoning helps me get through the day without dwelling too much on the dismembered dwarf, until it's time for me to go back to bed, and it starts all over again.

*

I held small jobs from the age of thirteen on, no longer to pay my mother's gambling debts, but, like all kids, to earn a little pocket money.

After selling ice cream for a few weeks on a bike — you remember those big white cubes mounted on tricycles — I was hired as a clerk in a video store located on boulevard Gouin inside the premises of the former Cinéma Commodore, whose death knell had been sounded by the rising popularity of VCRs.

I have fond memories of that job, at least until the owner demanded that I consult a psychiatrist at the Institut Albert-Prévost, situated just across the street.

At first, I felt deeply offended, but looking back I understand him. I had confessed to filming the murder of a dwarf and had threatened to screen the film on the video store's multiple TV monitors if he didn't raise my wages. He didn't appreciate my tone of voice, my insolence, and threatened to call the police if I refused to get professional help.

Rather than having the police march me out of the Commodore for a second time, I decided to go to Ravenscrag of my own accord; once there, I confided to a female colleague of Nab's that I was under the impression I'd killed and dismembered a dwarf, yet was unable to ascertain whether this event belonged to the world of dreams or the world of reality.

More than fifteen years on, I'm still waiting for an answer from the psychiatrist.

More than fifteen years on, I still wake up before the end.

*

I'm having trouble getting out of bed. For over two weeks now, though it may be months, I've lived in seclusion. I've had no news from Candice since she left the box full of documents on my balcony two days after her letter. No matter how much I go over them or try to give my mind a rest by summoning up pleasant memories, my brain keeps working overtime. I'm unable to get a grip, to control my thoughts, despite long hours devoted to breathing exercises.

The telephone rings several times a day, but I don't answer.

Most of the time I sit in the dark, except for the light of the cathode rays projected by the TV, which stays on day and night. One might assume that the glow bathes my apartment in tones of grey and white, but I'm among the very few owners of a colour TV on my street. It was the first item I bought after I was hired.

Because it's permanently turned on, I don't really pay attention to what's happening on the screen—the stories, the words. I enjoy in a very vague sort of way the flux of the rays or the perfectly cubic form of the device, the hue of its wooden surface, the small metal grid to the right of the screen, and the three large dials with which I would change channels before receiving my Jerrold from the U.S.

From time to time, I learn about developments in the outside world by peeking out through the hole in my blind, but I never keep this up for very long, given the reassuring constancy of the silhouette that keeps me under surveillance, day in day out, unfailingly: Salomé bides her time, lurking behind the tinted windows of her sedan.

*

My mind is not the only thing I'm losing. These past few days, I've had vision problems, blinding headaches, and luminous haloes coming between reality and me. To verify, I changed rooms; it's not the television.

When it became unbearable, I asked myself what my mother would do. After searching for a long time through her belongings, which were stored in the dirt-floor cellar below my apartment, I found her copy of *Mille secrets, mille dangers.* Self-diagnosis: scotomas due to stress and paranoia.

And what, you may be wondering, is a scotoma? It is an area of partial alteration in the field of vision, caused by the temporary absence of perception in a part of the retina. It produces all sorts of shapes: spirals, weird zigzags.

Holding my mother's only book in my hands took me back to our first trauma. Something broke between us then. I must have been four years old. She had gone out on an errand and left me with Sita, my Haitian nanny. When she returned, I knew that a wicked man had assumed my mother's features in order to harm me. From that day on I mistrusted her. She had been replaced.

After learning about Nab and Cameron, I fell into the habit of examining myself in the mirror to see if the same trick hadn't been played on me. What proof is there that I haven't been replaced, like my mother? How can I be certain that, during my naps, someone resembling my person wasn't substituted for me, so that I would be unable to detect the subterfuge, even if I tore off my own face?

★

Now I spend a good portion of my days repeating my name, my telephone number, my address. My name is Alain Farah, I can be reached at 514-289-6981, I live at 7310 Christophe Colomb, apartment 300, Montréal, Québec. I'm warming up for a far more important exercise: confirming that I am myself by answering private questions about my childhood.

In which neighbourhood did I grow up?

Cartierville, near Parc Belmont.

What role did I play in the staging of Christ's life at the orphanage?

John the Baptist.

Why did I wet my bed at night?

I was afraid Édouard would die one day.

Exactly when did I realize that my life would be complicated?

The first time I saw blood in my feces.

What colour was the spider that spun its web in a

corner of my bedroom, the spider that laid an egg in the centre of its web?

Orange body, green legs.

What happened to the spider?

It was devoured by the thousands of larvae that hatched from the egg.

My name is Alain Farah. I ate my mother. Everything is under control.

*

It was Édouard who drew me out of my lethargy. He forced the door to my apartment. The snow had melted, but I had no idea what month it was.

Édouard had started to worry after seeing nothing but the glow of the TV day after day. He called me every morning and evening, but I didn't answer. During the three weeks this routine went on for, he confined himself to watching me pace slowly back and forth between the bedroom and the living room, the bed and the couch, my nightmares and the disconnected images. After a month he became alarmed; it wasn't like me. He broke open the door. He found me in my pyjamas eating a bowl of cereal in bed. The room was littered with empty boxes and crushed cans. I was never big on housework, a trait that had a way of driving Candice mad. I closed the book by Carrère.

After a two-hour discussion, I agreed to go out. We took a few steps in the sunlight; it did us both good. After that, every day, Édouard came to visit and we would go for a walk. We called it "our little outing."

We repeated this exercise for five or six days. Meanwhile, spring came.

Earlier today, without realizing, I rediscovered an old habit, and when we arrived at our garage, I indulged myself with an electronic cigarette.

I felt it was the right moment, and I found the strength to tell my cousin about Cameron's implication in his father's death. I couldn't recognize my own voice. My cousin listened to me and shock soon gave way to equanimity; in response to my anger he argued that in any case his father was dead, that our turn would come, and we ought to make the best of whatever time was left by having fun. We couldn't bring him back, regardless.

Naturally, I disagreed. What was wrong with him? We would take revenge—period.

*

For over a week now I've been trying to persuade Édouard to avenge his father. The idea has begun to take root in his mind. My latest argument: this is our chance to finally cross over to the other side of the screen, our turn to act in the best film ever—the film of our lives.

This morning, during our planning session, Édouard pointed out a major stumbling block: "You want to avenge my father. Okay, but you aren't going to convince me that you know how to kill a man."

"I thought I would look it up in a book."

"Forget books. We'll go see the Italian. It'll be an opportunity for me to get paid. I've already sent him ten notices. Besides, I've heard that he's about to go back to Italy."

"Yes, Umberto must know how to get hold of a weapon."

"And on top of that, he's a scientist, isn't he?"

"Well, you know, anyone who's in literature is that to some extent."

"The other day, on TV, I saw that a dart gun is the most efficient way to eliminate someone inconspicuously. A small dart containing an infectious organism contaminates the victim's body. Think of it: injecting a deadly virus into Cameron's left thigh and having his CIA bosses believe it was an accident!"

"Do you have a quarter?"

★

An infectious organism... *hmm*. Easier said than done. As if we had time to spare. We'd need something swift and deadly: anthrax spores, smallpox-infected blankets, cologne tainted with mustard gas. But the only thing I might be able to rustle up in the short term would be a few E. coli from my daughter's daycare centre.

Note that if Umberto succeeds in getting his hands on a dart gun, Édouard could attach a small phial of midazolam to the tip of the dart and Cameron would get a taste of his own medicine.

I've been injected with this molecule ever since I was an adolescent, but after I was hired on at McGill, the dosage was steadily increased.

Without midazolam my life would be more predictable.

Take my last IV. The nurse in charge chatted with me practically all through the procedure. I think she found me interesting, with my books and my illnesses. I felt up to the conversation, even managing to crack a few jokes, yet at the same time I also felt terribly anxious. I felt as if our exchange wasn't registering in my brain, that the words were passing through me and were being recorded who knows where — in the mirror or in the brain of my replacement. The nurse realized that something was wrong and reassured me. At my prescribed dosage level, it was altogether natural for me to suffer from anterograde amnesia, a disturbance of the memory involving the inability to create new memories.

But memory had nothing to do with it. This was not my first IV, and I knew the side effects by heart. So I insisted. It was not about a memory disorder. It was my brain. It wasn't functioning normally: logic gone AWOL, proliferating identities, origami-like sense of time, intestinal anxiety, disjunctive logorrhoea. I had always been sickly, but this was a bit much. I asked to be given a bed for the night.

The doctors kept me under observation, but a hospital is no place to get a good night's sleep. Between having my vital signs checked every half hour and the nightmares induced by the sedatives, I hardly slept a wink.

At dawn, having finally dozed off, I had a strange dream in which the words "fortifications of Vauban" echoed endlessly in my head.

Why "fortifications of Vauban"? I have no idea.

When I stepped inside the elevator after being discharged, I bumped into the nurse again.

"I must say, Mr. Farah, you certainly are a garrulous one, you are. Under midazolam, people are usually quiet, or they confide their secrets to us. But you — a veritable lecture: Madame Bovary, the avant-gardes... We were almost tempted to take notes."

"Oh, I see. Did I tell you anything embarrassing while I was at it? I know we spoke at some length, but I have no recollection of it."

"I've never heard a patient with such a high dosage in his bloodstream speak so cogently. And as you spent the whole morning telling me you were a 'functioning madman,' I have no choice but to believe you."

"I hope I didn't dwell too long on the surrealists."

"In any case, it was quite entertaining, even though I didn't always follow you. Toward the end you spoke the same peculiar phrase over and over: 'Fortifications of Vauban.' You said it was the blind spot, the Bologna of Matamore. Oddly enough, you seemed aware of your derangement and would invariably begin your demonstration all over again, until, after a few sentences, the whole rigmarole repeated itself."

*

Umberto has asked us to meet him on the corner of chemin Upper Lachine and Melrose in the Notre-Dame-de-Grâce district, at a pastry shop displaying a long yellow plastic sign with, to the right of the bright red lettering, images of a sausage, a wheel of parmesan, a knuckle of ham, and a reversed Italian flag. The tomatoes they use in the pizza here are delicious.

The little bells over the front door chime as Édouard and I step inside. The Italian, leaning on the counter, is sipping an espresso and talking with the owner's daughter. Could it be his guilty desire for this fourteen-year-old girl that makes him tense up when he sees us? However that may be, Umberto is on the defensive: "*Bello, come vai?*

Ah, you've dropped in with your cousin... The Nozze have come to pay me a visit. You're here to talk money with me."

"Don't start, you two, with your money issues. I'm willing to pay what you owe my cousin if you'll help me out a little."

"Why would you pay his debt? He's got plenty of money, this guy, with the chair he holds in Italy. Besides, I've been sending him invoices for months now."

"Would you please let me finish, Édouard? Umberto, if you can pull a few strings for me concerning something a bit on the shady side, I'll pay for your damn repair job."

"What did I say? The Nozze pop up and, hello, it's the collection agency."

Édouard, usually a calm man, doesn't find this very funny.

"Why do you call us Nozze?"

"Your family name is Farah, right?"

"My name is Safi, which you would know if you had bothered to open the fucking bills."

"I'm playing on words, here, Eddy, relax. Allow me to explain: *farah*, in Arabic, means marriage, and marriage, in Italian, is *nozze*..."

"To think that you're paid a fortune to spout this sort of drivel, while I knock myself out for eighty dollars a week at the garage."

Umberto doesn't appreciate my cousin's comment.

"Oh, so now you're going to chastise me for not waging the class struggle."

I ask the young waitress for a coffee. Then I interrupt the Italian, looking him in the eye: "I need a weapon."

"*Bello*, what's the matter? Are you in trouble?"

I pay for my coffee without hurrying and without saying another word. Umberto understands that I won't be elaborating.

"Okay, okay, I won't ask you why. In any event, I'm flying to Rome tonight. Do whatever you like, I just need to make a phone call."

*

Three quarters of an hour later, Umberto finally reappears from the back of the shop. His demeanour suggests that he's proud of what he's about to tell us.

I wolf down the rest of my cannoli.

"I spoke to a cousin of mine. I let him know it was a matter of some urgency, and he came up with what seems to be a fairly solid plan. This guy you want to bump off — we'll call him the Turk — invite him to a good restaurant and engage him in a quiet conversation."

"What about?"

"Anything at all, it doesn't matter: ask how his wife is, talk about the menu, suggest the veal, something with a biblical touch to it, a sacrificial touch. Then — my cousin stressed this — you'll switch to Italian, but with no subtitles."

Édouard breaks in: "What do you mean, no subtitles?"

I turn toward my cousin. "He doesn't want the viewers to understand. It heightens the suspense of the scene, a narratologist's trick. These things can't be explained in a couple of minutes. Let him finish, hold your questions for later."

Umberto concurs: "*Exactemente . . . Ciao* to the subtitles, and then you dolly the camera back from the table, to give the scene more breadth. You can see the décor, the guests, the waitresses, *e tutti quanti*. You drink some wine, you let a few minutes go by, you rub your stomach, you grimace with pain. Everyone knows about stomach aches."

"But you always tell me not to talk about your illness," Édouard cuts in.

I signal impatiently with my hand for him to drop it, this isn't the right time.

"Go on, Umberto."

"The Turk won't be surprised that you need to go to the toilet. If he has any suspicions, he can just search you, you won't be carrying anything."

"Yes, but isn't the whole point of all this to get hold of a handgun?"

"*Pazienza!* You head toward the washroom, taking your time. When you get to the last stall you remove the lid from the tank. That's where the gun is, wrapped in a plastic bag. You take it, go back to your seat, take a deep breath, and then, *pow! pow!* You put two bullets in your guy's head."

*

After enjoying Umberto's pantomime of the scene—it's so intense and moving that the owner's daughter chokes on her Chinotto—I say:

"I don't know where your cousin got this idea, Umberto, but the individual I have to take down isn't someone who readily accepts dinner invitations. And I won't have very much time to…."

Édouard interrupts, speaking directly to Umberto: "Don't you think a dart gun would be a better choice?"

Umberto raises his hands. "You wanted a gun. I found you a gun. What else can I say?"

I glare at my cousin.

"Please forgive us. Put it down to nervousness. But the man who's out to hurt us—it would take a precision rifle to shoot him down."

Édouard clears his throat emphatically. I ignore him.

"Er, Alain?"

"Yes, Édouard."

"The thing is, I was wondering. Will you be able to adopt the prone position when you shoot?"

"That's it? That's your question?"

"Enough of your foolishness," Umberto cuts in. "I'll come along with you to my cousin's place. We'll see what he can do."

★

I don't exactly expect Umberto to take us a Cosa Nostra gunsmith, but when we leave his cousin's house with a toy gun I tell myself we got our wires crossed. For all I know, it's a water pistol.

"For heaven's sake, *bello*, this is not a toy! Why would my cousin palm off a toy on you?"

"I may not be an expert on guns, but even so, Umberto. The thing weighs barely a few ounces, it's made of plastic, and your cousin never mentioned ammunition."

"Not to contradict you," Édouard breaks in, "but this is probably a non-conventional weapon moulded out of revolutionary synthetic polymers. Its toy-like appearance is meant to dupe the enemy. This type of gun is so sophisticated it doesn't even require projectiles. Everything is activated when you pull the trigger. Cause and effect occur simultaneously. This is advanced technology, so, naturally, it doesn't weigh anything."

I don't know about you, but I find what Édouard has to say quite convincing. After all, he's the mechanic. I decide that he's right, and we head out toward McGill. Édouard and I say very little while Umberto tells us about his latest conquests. I would be less than truthful if I denied being somewhat apprehensive at the thought of facing Cameron with a weapon whose workings are beyond my grasp. I'm counting on Candice—I spoke with her for a long time on the telephone at the back of the pastry shop earlier—to give me a hand. I need a Plan B, an emergency exit, an exfiltration strategy. You never know how these situations will turn out.

Something of Candice's voice has stayed in my ears, and there's no better antidote to the voices haunting my brain. I need to see her again. If I had listened to Candice from the very start, if I had taken my bath like the others, perhaps none of this would have happened.

*

We arrive at the office.

The four of us gather around the conference table in a large room in the Arts Building. Candice, standing with both hands pressed flat on the tabletop, is in command. The milder weather has brought a change of wardrobe, and my heart clenches at the sight of her moving in a diaphanous silk blouse and a royal blue sheath skirt that hugs her waist. What about footwear? Boots? No, Candice steps lightly and wears ballet shoes.

The whole room is lit up by a diagram that she has placed on a powerful overhead projector to illustrate her plan: "We'll have to take advantage of the element of surprise. Alain, you say that the entrances to Ravenscrag have been sealed, is that correct?"

She removes the useless sunglasses from the top of her head and places them near her on the conference table.

"Yes, the watchman said that security procedures have been tightened. I believe this was in response to your intrusion into their data banks."

"Which means there is only one way to reach Cameron: you must go through the McTavish reservoir. I've pulled some strings and secured an authorization from the system supervisors. You'll be able to access the site at 815 McGregor."

"Excellent. So what are we waiting for?"

Candice can't suppress a knowing smile, the kind that says, "You'll never change."

"Not so fast. The last time you were in my office you left something behind, next to my desk. A pillbox."

"Yes, as I explained over the phone, it contained the capsules that Cameron had given me."

"Precisely what I was afraid of. I had the pillbox analyzed at the biochemistry lab. There was still some residue from the capsules inside. The results are inconclusive, but I suspect that Cameron had given you a magistral preparation containing a derivative of barbiturates that induces memory disjunctions in patients when they come into contact with water."

"But I haven't taken any of those capsules in weeks."

"The molecule's half-life can be months after the treatment has ended. Cameron is one of the world's foremost psychiatrists, at the cutting edge of current research in a number of fields, from pharmacology to philosophy. He has read the article that the young French philosopher Michel Foucault just published in *Médecine et Hygiène*. The mechanism of action developed by Cameron is exactly in line with Foucault's hypothesis."

Umberto, probably busy fabricating alibis to cover up his Montreal infidelities, comes back down to earth when he hears the name of his French colleague.

Édouard, who took the journal from Candice's desk, reads a passage from the article out loud: "Water, in the asylum, leads back to the naked truth. Violently lustrous, it operates simultaneously both at the baptism and the confession. By taking the patient back to the time before the fall, it forces him to recognize himself for what he is."

"That's exactly what happens to me. I can't go out in the rain without being swamped with memories."

"Which means that when you go into the reservoir," Candice says, "the very high flow rate in the vicinity of the pumps will trigger a series of reminiscences even more dizzying than the previous ones. According to my calculations, there is even a risk that you experience memories other than your own, of events that slightly preceded your birth."

"Have your calculations told you if the memories are pleasant?"

*

If avenue McGregor still existed, pedestrians passing in front of the medieval-castle-style pumping station would no doubt wonder what on earth a grieving mechanic, a flirtatious semiologist, a Huguenot researcher, and a mythomaniac at the end of his rope might be up to, standing around in a circle like football players huddling before the next down.

Actually, it's quite simple. Umberto is adjusting my goggles. Candice is loosening my tie and reminding me to be wary of Cameron until the very end: "It's when he appears to be at your mercy that he'll potentially be the most dangerous." Édouard, meanwhile, gives me a bear hug and discreetly whispers in my ear: "Be strong, cousin. Don't forget, the effect is in the cause, the projectile is in the trigger."

"I don't like it when you tell me things like that. You're confusing me. The gun—will it work or not?"

"It all depends on you."

Before I open the huge solid wood doors at the base of the square tower, I say goodbye to my confederates. Then I step inside the building.

. I picture them returning to their occupations.

Candice, back in her office, worried sick about me but believing in my success; Édouard, behind the wheel of his car, driving the Italian to the airport; Umberto, coming through customs, waving to his waiting wife, now six months pregnant.

*

Oakwood moulding climbs up to the ceiling, which is banded with joists fashioned out of the same wood. I step toward a copper door fitted with the small window typical of elevators in the 1930s and surmounted by the City of Montreal's coat of arms comprising a fleur-de-lys, a lion, and a maple leaf. The windows to the left and right of the copper-plated door look onto the vast halls where, as Candice informed me, colossal pumps are at work.

I enter the elevator, which takes me down three floors to a grey control panel worthy of a spaceship, with multi-coloured levers, dials, and buttons.

I open the interconnecting gates that will allow me to go through the four concrete tanks built inside the massive chamber that was carved into the belly of mont Royal.

I ride down past the pumps and find myself several stories below ground, in one of the thousands of valve houses of the city. I make my way among conduits each one metre across; the flow of water inside them is such that when I place my hand on their rusted surface I feel a tremendous rumble.

Fortunately, the darkness isn't pitch-black. There are slender shafts of light streaming down through the manhole covers at the surface of avenue McGregor. But the awareness of being so far underground sets off pangs of anxiety that make my face go numb. To calm down, I focus on moving forward.

*

With the last channel now behind me, I come to the main vault of the edifice. Before me rises a tank twenty metres high containing several hundred million gallons of water.

In 1931, the place where I'm standing was the submerged bottom of the reservoir. When it was covered over, concrete tanks were erected inside the space occupied by the original basin, thereby creating an antechamber, a passage between the new and the old structures of the reservoir.

Candice clearly explained to me that, to get from one tank to the next, I first need to skirt the reservoir by going along either the concrete wall that contains the reservoir water or the underground rock face dripping with the overflow from the water table.

Craning my neck to the utmost, I examine the series

of tanks that, like Russian dolls, sit one inside the other right up to the Ravenscrag swimming pool.

I walk almost touching the rock face, which is covered in some places with green moss, in others with chalk, and still elsewhere with a layer of metal oxide that gives the rock a coppery tinge. Here and there, the water trickles down the rock and puddles at my feet. Then, as the corridor widens and forks, I reach an iron staircase that leads to a vaulted, brick-lined passage closed off by a wire-mesh gate.

I climb three steps and open the gate. It's warmer inside the tunnel. I loosen my tie even more. I'm obliged to stoop and bend my knees as I walk.

It's pitch-dark now. A distant sound of croaking reaches my ears. Some ravens have taken up residence in the last little section of the passage, which is not under water. At least I'm not alone.

I balk at taking another step, fearing it may be my last. A shiver runs through my whole body, wrenching me out of my thoughts. Nothing exists anymore except the mouth of this tank. I perceive its existence concretely, discerning alterations in quasi-molecular detail, as if I were pointing an ultra-high-powered zoom lens at its steel surface.

This is it.

I cross myself and plunge into the first tank of the reservoir.

*

The water engulfs me at a staggering rate, and we've been tramping through the bush for hours now, my children and I. My daughter walks at a steady pace, sometimes stopping to catch an insect or to pick flowers of many different colours. But my son's haggard eyes tell me it's time to find a shelter where we can rest. He looks bone-tired.

This forked tree will do.

With my daughter in the lead, we climb one behind the other up toward the middle of the majestic broad-leaved tree; once there, we make ourselves at home.

I never sleep so soundly as when I'm perched in a tree, but my son's crying pulls me out of my REM sleep. The silence of the night has just been rent by a prodigious trumpeting sound. My son is so terrified that he has trouble speaking.

"Do you think a monster made that noise, Dad?"

"You know perfectly well that monsters live under children's bed and in closets, not in the brush. Go back to sleep."

I stretch my hand out to his branch and stroke his hair. After he drifts off, I turn back toward the meadows where an inquisitive herd of brachiosaurs are watching us.

I make all sorts of odd gestures so that they don't wake my kids, but to no avail. My panicked children are shaking like leaves and whispering that they're going to be devoured.

"Calm down, for God's sake. Brachiosaurs are herbivores, everyone knows that."

Émilie is reassured and explains to her little brother that, despite being thirty metres long and having a four-storey neck, brachiosaurs are a very peaceful species of dinosaur, like giant cows, possibly the biggest animals ever to have set foot on the face of the planet.

I add: "We're privileged to experience such a wonderful moment together as a family. Lots of people would pay a fortune to see such beasts up close." I tear a small branch off our tree and call out to these reptiles of the past: "Come on, little buddies! Come on! Come see daddy Alain!"

Two brachiosaurs move toward us with slow, heavy steps and let us stroke the tips of their snouts. My children, looking both petrified and softened at the same time, their heads smaller than one of these giants' nostrils, pet them ever so gently.

The next day we climb down from the tree and cross a sweeping meadow. Dozens of gallimimuses come in our direction. Émilie asks me if they are carnivores, to which I answer: "Don't worry, princess, dinosaurs don't eat meat."

No sooner have I finished my sentence than the Jurassic hens become agitated and suddenly change directions. An approaching predator? In the distance, a tyrannosaurus does in fact come into view and bears down on the gallimimuses with frightening speed, snaps one up in its jaws and rips off the head in a spray of tendons and blood. Fortunately, along with the horrific biped, I catch sight of the interconnecting channel that will convey me to the second tank.

*

I'm still in possession of all my limbs, in itself reason enough to rejoice and allow myself a short break.

The channel that joins the tanks is two metres across—not exactly comfortable but at least I can keep my head above water.

How many people have already found themselves in this situation, all alone in the world, in transit between two gigantic tanks, on the way to meeting their uncle's murderer, armed with a gun that is either lethal or harmless (I'll learn soon enough, though possibly at my own expense)?

That said, if I come out of this story alive, I'm going to share it with a few reporters. It should be good for a few headlines: WRITER SURVIVES DINOSAUR ATTACK; CLOSE ENCOUNTER OF THE FOURTH KIND IN THE BELLY OF THE MCTAVISH RESERVOIR; CAMERON'S KILLER TELLS ALL, etc.

I'm joking, but they are useful—newspapers, that

is — I can attest to that. Last year, for instance, the daily *Le Devoir* invited me to write a sports column. Since this was a one-off, the section editor had a short bio note appended to my piece. In it, I made a point of mentioning that I was conducting an inquiry into the links between McGill and the CIA. It was like a message in a bottle. Well, the following day, at dawn, my publisher received a call from a victim of Cameron, wishing to contact me and tell her story.

At first I was sure it was a hoax cooked up by Umberto or Édouard, so I didn't reply to Mrs. Blouin — let's call her that — but a few days later I caught myself thinking, "Now what if it's true?" The prospect of meeting Mrs. Blouin didn't particularly disturb me; she did, after all, subscribe to a respectable daily newspaper. But I wavered and worried about not knowing what to do with her narrative, especially because, every time we talked on the telephone, the lady emphasized the large number of documents she wanted to give me. My intuition would be confirmed. The person I met turned out to be a cheerful woman and an outstanding storyteller, who entertained me for an afternoon at her charming house in Beloeil on Montreal's South Shore, tastefully decorated despite her blindness.

For three hours, I listened to her discuss the existence of God and the Devil, reiki and the planet Mars, the traumas of childhood and of depatterning. The strangest thing about our conversation, however, was that her husband, who was down in the basement playing on a Nintendo console, never came up to say hello, behaviour I find not so much rude as inappropriate.

Speaking of God and the Devil, it's time for me to move on to the second tank. Once again, I cross myself and jump in, with, on the other side, Christ waiting for me on the banks of the Jordan River—you never know.

*

The flow is not as overwhelming as that of the previous tank; still, the blasts of water lash at my face, and I always feel sick when I'm at sea. It wasn't a good idea to go out for a stroll on the deck. Let's go back inside and take a look around the ship. Oh, some more animals: chickens, hogs, even horses are being kept in pens. I'd never given it much thought, but you do have to eat while crossing the Atlantic, and there are no freezers.

This occurred to me because of the man sitting next to me in the mess. We've been talking for about an hour, and I've almost managed to forget the pitch of the vessel and the smell of iodine and boiled cabbage.

My neighbour at the table tells me that he just left his hometown, Glasgow, with a head full of plans, and he's eager to arrive in the New World. But he'd rather not dwell on it, as it'll be another three weeks before we reach Montreal. I gulp and try desperately to see through the dark water of the second tank if the hatchway of the next interconnecting channel is in sight, but in vain.

With James — the man's given name — I adopt the relaxed and interested attitude of an airplane passenger chatting with the individual that chance has seated beside him. James, then, confides to me that he intends to engage in the fur trade once he lands in the colony. He plans to sail the Great Lakes, become a prosperous merchant, selling munitions and all manner of merchandise. Very soon — I love this about the English language — we're on a first-name basis: "What is your dream, James?"

"One day, I shall buy myself a farm of forty-six acres and foster the creation of a system of education in Lower Canada, and I'll found the Royal Institution for the Advancement of Science."

"But what's the connection between the farm and the educational system?"

"My farm, located on the slopes of mont Royal, will be an ideal site to build a college bearing my name, provided the Americans don't try to invade us again and there's not too much dithering before William the Fourth signs our institution's charter."

"And when do you see this happening?"

"If all goes as planned, McGill College will open its doors on the feast day of St. John the Baptist in 1829. A few years on, just opposite the McTavish reservoir, we'll erect the Arts Building, where, if all goes as planned, you'll one day have your office."

*

The steep incline of the next interconnecting channel rushes me from the eighteenth century to the penultimate tank without even letting me catch my breath. An autumn chill pierces me to the bone. I know this place. I'm on what used to be James's farm, who-knows-how-many decades after we met on the high seas.

The water has reconstituted me in the middle of a huge rally right in the heart of the city. To the west and east of the Roddick Gates, as far as my eyes can see, rue Sherbrooke is overflowing with people. I realize that I'm among a small group waving signs. I ask a young man wearing a mask in the likeness of an English conspirator: "Excuse me, what's going on here? Why are so many people gathered in front of McGill?"

"The premier's office is directly across the street! We're going to tell Charest to his face that we want none of his tuition fee hike!"

My only response is a silly smile, because I don't want to annoy this fellow, who's obviously under the influence of drugs. Ordinarily, Montreal demonstrations involve no more than a few hundred people.

The small group next to me gathers in a circle. I hear

everything. A girl with a red *keffiyeh* tied around her neck says it's time to carry out the plan, the media have put the number of protestors at two hundred thousand, it's now or never, there's hardly any security in front of the James Building.

I chime in: "The university's administrative nerve centre — excellent idea. I'm familiar with the place. I could show you how to get to the principal's office; I was invited there when I was hired. There's even a musket — kept under a bell glass — that once belonged to McGill!"

I sense the discomfort of some members of the group, but the leader settles it: if I'm an agent provocateur, I'll be exposed soon enough, there's no time for discussion, the word has already spread among the comrades, the rest of the demo will come support us in front of the designated building.

We reach the fifth floor of the building. My membership in the crew is no longer in doubt; I'm the one who gives the signal to unfurl the banner that Ernesto made earlier today. It reads: 10 NOV. OCCUPY MCGILL.

We're prepared for a long occupation. But a few minutes after the release of our communiqué, a dozen security agents storm the principal's office hollering, "We have a visual on the insurgents!"

Am I the one who betrayed my comrades without realizing?

We dash down the stairs to the ground floor, but it's

a mistake. A hundred helmeted police are waiting for us in the square in front of the James Building. They repeatedly strike their shields with their batons, producing a deafening drumbeat for the squad's advance.

A helicopter circles slowly overhead. From inside the cabin, a commander, shouting through a megaphone, pronounces these words: "This demonstration is illegal. You must disperse." He has hardly finished when the police on the ground begin to pepper-spray us. While some comrades are being driven back to the bottom of the slope, I raise my hands in the air and yell that I give up.

The blast of stun grenades rocks the air three times, the crowd scatters under the effect of the irritant gas, and the use of force to rid the campus of protestors progresses from one stage to the next: communication, moderate physical control, intense physical control, intermediate weapons. That's where things stand now.

The final stage before "use of lethal force" is rubber bullets. As I don't wish to lose an eye, I start running along Milton toward avenue du Parc. The cavalry has blocked all the intersections to the north and south.

I make my escape through the final interconnecting channel.

★

The conduit is large enough for me to stand up straight. I can take stock of the damage this strange swim has done to my skin. Did Candice predict that my passage through the first three tanks would cause this severe redness? How many years have I been submerged for my skin to pucker like this?

I hesitate to heave myself up to the mouth of the interconnecting channel, because, once inside the last tank, that is, immersed in the Ravenscrag swimming pool, it will be too late for me to back out of my plan.

How does one go about killing a man in real life?

For the last time, I examine the polymer gun that's been slung across my shoulder from the Cretaceous to the principal's office. Once again, I have doubts about its effectiveness, especially since Édouard's discourse shifted from mechanics to faith. Help thy gun and thy gun will help thee — that's a good one. I should have trusted my instincts, gotten a precision weapon, and convinced Umberto's cousin to let me shoot Cameron at a distance, in the back, or whatever, anything to avoid having to talk to him. Candice's warning gnaws at me: it's when he claims to be weak that he'll be strongest.

Have you read Jean-Patrick Manchette? He's the author of some excellent crime novels, including *The Prone Gunman*, my favourite book of his. As the novel progresses from one page to the next, Manchette settles accounts once and for all with cookie-cutter plots. In the end, the writer transforms his hero, Martin Terrier, the best hit man of his generation, into a waiter in a pub somewhere in the French Ardennes. It's as if the narrator at the end of the novel in Hubert Aquin's *Next Episode*, rather than blowing his brains out on the grounds of the Villa Maria, decided to get a job at the convenience store across the street and to spend the rest of his life fantasizing over pictures of Grace Kelly in *Paris Match*. As for me, it's not that I've abandoned the hand-to-hand combat with narration; the fact is I've been playing chess for thirty years and never won a single game. Writing is a game, and when you play you lose.

Do we ever get used to telling stories that don't work?

In other versions of this book, the events unfolded without a break. It was seamless: I opened and closed a lot of doors, I moved characters from one scene to the next, in a word: boring. In one scene, Candice clipped her fingernails and then filed them. What's more, it was tedious to write, so I erased the whole thing. Otherwise, what's the point? I prefer to tinkle out a few tunes I find enjoyable, even if there are fewer of you on the dance floor.

*

But I digress, I delay. Obviously, I could cross the interconnecting channel in an instant, but now that the end
of the road is in sight, I feel like going back to my start-
ing point.

I was just putting the final touches on this episode
when it occurred to me to phone Capucine to invite
her to the Faculty Club, the posh nineteenth-century
house reserved for McGill professors. I have my routine there: hello, good to see you, club sandwich, iced
tea, the bill.

On the telephone, Capucine avers that my call surprises her. The last time we met, it was in another world,
at Léa-Catherine's house, six or seven years ago.

"Precisely!"

"Precisely what?"

"You remember the Italian who came on to you
under the pergola? I wanted to include that anecdote
in my book, but if you don't recall it I won't be able to
because there would be no one to confirm the veracity
of what I'm writing."

"Oh, I see. Say goodbye to authenticity. Is that it?"

"Yes, it makes things quite complicated."

"Shit. Can I be in you book anyway? If nothing else,
write 'crossbow' or 'grapefruit' and I'll know it's meant
for me."

"Unfortunately, that won't be possible. After *Matamore no 29*, my last novel, a bookseller told me, 'Your book is a party, but we're not on the guest list.'"

"To tell you the truth, I didn't understand a word of it."

"I know, and you're not alone. Well, in my next one, there'll be no more obscure allusions, a clear timeline, no ellipses or digressions, complex characters with varied, subtle motivations, finely wrought prose, and a relentless plot. I'm fed up with my publisher's complaints. I want to produce a normal novel. That said, I may lend Candice a hint of levity."

"Yes! And could she also have three cats: a black cat, a grey cat, and a ginger cat?"

"Right. Candice has three cats: black, grey, and ginger."

*

I stay near the bottom of the Ravenscrag swimming pool by slowly rotating my arms and legs. I am a crocodile, a blobfish, phytoplankton. I'm waiting for something to happen to me, but the pressure on my ears is too strong, so I rise to the surface, letting only my eyes emerge above the water. I carefully scan the environs. Seeing no one, I swim over to the steps of the pool, which I mount in a single bound.

As I walk toward the metal door, the wet slap of my feet echoes under the room's vaulted ceiling. I'm about to open it when, from behind, a familiar voice makes me jump.

"I had a feeling we were not done with you, Professor."

Diop, elegantly attired in a yellow silk kimono tied at the waist, seems to be amused by my arrival. His face is paler than ever, as though bleached by chlorine.

"You see, it was a bad idea for you to come back. Miss Cameron was telling me the other day how very poor your powers of reasoning are. He is obsessed, she said, and will try everything to contact my father. God knows what is going on inside his head. I think you will appreciate the few small changes we have made just to keep you here with us."

"You're making threats even though I'm holding a weapon?"

"You are referring to that toy? It probably shoots nothing but water, if that."

"Is that so? I said the very same thing the first time I saw this gun."

"I am not surprised. Have you never realized how much we resemble each other?"

"You're not actually going to tell me that you're my father, are you?"

"No, I shall leave that sort of thing to space opera villains. But I do owe you a few words of explanation as to the ties that bind us."

Diop is about to expound but is stopped in his tracks by my next move. He is less surprised than me, whose understanding of things always lags behind, as if one half of me acted without informing the other half.

It all happened in a matter of seconds. I clasped the gun in both hands, stretched out my arms and raised it to eye level as if aiming, a ridiculous reflex, because I simultaneously squeezed them shut—my eyes, that is. With the gun pointed vaguely in Diop's direction, I shouted in a strangely metallic voice: "Take this, you lowlife! The effect is in the cause, the projectile is in the trigger!"

I look at Diop, sprawled on the ground. I was wrong to doubt. The damage inflicted by my gun is astonishing. The watchman, stone cold dead, grows more and more pale. By degrees, his face becomes other faces, successively taking on the features of Montaigne Racine, my old friend at the orphanage, then of Christian Loubaki a.k.a. Enfant Mystère, servant to Sir Hugh Allan and inventor of La Sape, and, finally, those of a third, oddly familiar face, which I'm unable to identify.

I kneel beside Diop's corpse and begin to rub the skin on his face. I must get to the bottom of this, but my face goes more numb than ever. No matter—I keep on rubbing. The black shoe polish that he'd used to darken his skin gradually fades, revealing features that elude all identity, as when a mirror is cleaned to the point where the reflection itself is wiped out.

*

On the other side of the steel door, Ravenscrag is beyond recognition. Gone are the spiral stairways, the black marble, the thirty-six chambers. The mansion has been transformed, reduced to a single, endless, horizontally dizzying corridor, which I have no choice but to walk down, not knowing what awaits me at the far end.

How could Cameron have so altered this place since my last visit? Could Ravenscrag be made not of stone but of the same polymer as my toy gun? Can its structure be remodelled according to our desires, like Plasticine or language, the ultimate plastic?

I march steadily toward who knows what, but my accelerating pulse is a sign that the corridor is on a slight upward incline. I hold my weapon tight against my chest and try to think of nothing; otherwise I would freeze in an aimless panic and be incapable of taking another step.

*

I've been making my way along the dimly lit corridor for a good hour when I finally perceive what I believe to be the end. In front of something that looks like a door I can distinguish a motionless silhouette. At a distance of no more than thirty metres, I soon recognize Salomé, Salomé Cameron.

"This is where your story comes to a close, Farah, assuming it has ever begun."

This of course is not a good time to compliment her, but I notice her outfit, a gothic iteration of the classic little black dress, edged, just above the knees, with fur.

"It's rabbit," she says.

"Excuse me?"

"You hesitate to talk about my dress, but go ahead. That's all women are for you anyway: coat hangers, faces to be made up, moving pictures. You're pathetic."

"I couldn't have said it better myself."

"You've wasted enough of our time."

"Your dress reminds me of something... Isn't it the one Anna Karina wears at the end of *Alphaville?*"

"As I was saying, a pathetic little man who worships box-office flops. Despite your fondness for allusions, you didn't even take the trouble to understand my warning. If you had read the book I gave you more carefully, if you had listened more closely to the recording I brought you, you wouldn't be standing here like a laboratory rat about to have its brain fried."

A few of the verses reprinted in the liner notes of the Wu-Tang Clan album come back to me. I recite them for Salomé: *"When I was little, my father was famous / He was the greatest samurai in the empire, and he was the Shogun's decapitator / He cut off the heads of a hundred and thirty-one lords..."*

A look of sadness floats across her face, and she continues: "'*The shogun just stayed inside his castle ... his brain was infected by devils.*' We could go on like this for a long time, but it's no good living in the past."

"Are you going to cut off my head, Salomé?"

"The frightening thing about the present is that it is irreversible. Cut off your head? Ha, ha, ha! You and your Biblical references. I'm going to do far worse than that."

Without waiting for the details, I shut my eyes and point my gun at her, shouting the same words as those I pronounced earlier to Diop. The results are the same. Salomé collapses on the floor, but not without repeating, "I'm going to do far worse than that."

★

I don't know how Salomé managed it, but I find myself in Édouard's garage, amid the mechanical noise of a hydraulic lift. We're about to install a distributor belt on a neighbour's Passat.

After a few minutes' work, we stop for a break. I show my cousin my electronic cigarette with a USB charger that lets my entire Rolodex know in real time that I'm smoking an "American blend." He borrows it from me to try it out and takes three or four long puffs as he goes back to the car. Suddenly, he stops, letting the cigarette drop on the ground. He complains of sharp pains in his back. He takes deep breaths while I rush to get him a glass of water.

When I come back, he says he's feeling better, but a moment later he starts vomiting.

"Let's go back to my apartment. You can lie down in my bedroom. You must have caught a virus."

"I don't think so. I've been having backaches for months. Can I take a shower?"

"Of course, but shouldn't you get some sleep instead?"

"Hot water is the only thing that helps. I think my blood vessels dilate when I dunk myself in boiling water. It helps the circulation."

"Shouldn't we call an ambulance?"

"I really don't feel like going to the hospital. Seriously. Not after what happened to my father."

While my cousin is in the shower, I waffle over calling the paramedics. However, when he steps out of the bathroom, I beg him to let me dial 911. He has a greenish colour and admits that the pain has returned with a vengeance. He agrees, and the ambulance arrives barely five minutes after I place the call.

The two members of the ambulance team install Édouard in my bed and place several machines around him. Not wanting to interfere, I don't dare ask any questions, but I believe they're running an ECG. After looking over the test results, one of the paramedics, a woman around thirty years old, tells Édouard: "Sir, your heart is giving out. We're going to the Institut de Cardiologie. You have to see a doctor right away."

The look Édouard gives me at this point is horrifying. As they wheel him out of the house on the stretcher, he pulls away his oxygen mask and says, "If anything happens to me, will you take care of my children?"

I'm incapable of the slightest response.

The paramedics take him to the ambulance and speed away.

Back in my kitchen, I go around in circles, unable to make a decision no matter how simple. The telephone jangles me out of my inertia. I don't answer; instead, I go to my bedroom, where Édouard's T-shirt is still lying on the floor.

*

When I awake, I'm in the middle of an immense black cube whose dimensions are impossible to ascertain, that's how hazy the lighting is in the room.

It's neither hot nor cold.

Instinctively, the first thing I do is check whether I still have my gun strapped across my shoulder. It's gone.

Cameron's voice, resonant and metallic, rings out inside the cube from everywhere at once, with no discernable point of origin; he's humming the mournful song that Jean Lapointe sings at the end of *Les Ordres*: "*Écoutez mon histoire jeune homme qui a voyagé / La mort peut apparaître sans que vous l'attendiez / Avec sa main de traître elle pourrait vous frapper*. Those are the lyrics, Farah, aren't they?"

I raise my head and answer the voice issuing from an unknown location: "I wasn't expecting to discuss our folk tradition with you."

"Why? Don't you enjoy cultural exchanges? You are wearing a tie with a Double Windsor knot, so why can't I sing '*La complainte à mon frère*'?"

Cameron appears before me. If it weren't for the strange force pinning me down, I could reach him in two strides.

"You don't have the same name as your uncle, but you have the same despicable foibles. Forever sticking your nose in other people's business."

Tormented by a harrowing headache, I nevertheless manage to respond: "Perhaps, but at least I have the courage to be here. You took advantage of Nab's weakness and finished him off when he was worn down by illness."

"I'm surprised, I must admit, that you've been able to cope without the capsules. But I was right to believe in you. Soon my primary mission will be accomplished: to destroy you and turn you into someone else."

"You're out of your mind, Cameron. All these years

spent depatterning people have taken their toll on you."

"You're right, I feel the end is at hand. I was intending to let my daughter take over the laboratory, but when I realized you were seeking revenge, I told myself this would be my final project."

"What are you talking about?"

"When you reached the corner of University and avenue des Pins, you didn't go see that flunky, Penfield. You turned left, you came to me, because you knew I was the only one who could give you a story."

"You think I've done all this just to have a story to tell?"

"No, that was a poor choice of words. I should have said, 'who could give you back your story.' Because, after all, Ravenscrag is your home as much as mine. Maybe you had forgotten it; all I did was to refresh your memory. Which proves that I treat you differently from the others; as a rule, memory is something I erase."

"You believe that you're powerful, Cameron, but the only people you control are weak and on the verge of breaking down."

"I prefer to be on the side of power than on the side of idiocy, Professor. You prefer to go begging for a little love from everyone, by doing tricks for anyone who asks. You don't understand the larger context. I got rid of your uncle because he was incapable of seizing the chance he'd been given and of taking advantage of this new power: to get inside people's heads, to control them, destroy them, reconstruct them."

"Writing books is quite enough for me."

"Let me know if, with your books, you're able to endure what I have in store for you."

Cameron, who has come closer and closer as we played out our exchange, whispers these last words in my ear. Now he takes a step back.

Despite being a small man, he makes a sweeping theatrical gesture toward one wall of the cube, which turns into a screen. The picture projected is of me.

*

I find myself in the back of an ambulance, but the person I'm with is not Édouard. I'm accompanying my mother, who is feeling not at all well. Her eyes wide open, she squeezes my hand.

The paramedics tell me that they are losing her, that there's not enough time to get to the Institut de Cardiologie, they'll have to stop at the Hôpital du Sacré-Coeur.

Her lungs are full of water, she's having a massive heart attack, and the team at the hospital is already preparing the operating room.

When we reach Sacré-Coeur, the specialist talks to me about aortic valve replacement, ascending aorta replacement, coronary artery bypasses. I don't understand a word he's saying. In any case, all I want to know is, can they save her.

The questions collide with each other in my head: How do you manage, Cameron, to put me through things like this? What were the chances of both my mother and my cousin having heart attacks, just like Nab, before I even finished my book about you? How can *that* be explained?

He answers me from inside his black cube behind the screen: "You don't know what you've gotten yourself into, Farah. You could pass through the screen again and come within close range of me. I'm even ready to give you back your gun; you could train it on me. Whether you spare me or put a bullet in my head would make no difference—I've already won."

"What are you talking about? Now that I've found you, I'm going to destroy you, burn down your mansion, liberate your patients."

"You mean your patients, Farah. You're so pitifully naive. Take a good look at the other side of the screen, make yourself comfortable in front of your favourite series, it's about to begin."

*

There's no one but me in the black cube.

This is intergalactic space. There's no need to hide

anywhere. Space belongs to me and so does the big black cube. All your base are belong to us!

Snugly ensconced in my armchair, I activate the intercom and broadcast my voice throughout city, from the Saint-Laurent to the rivière des Prairies.

"*En l'an 2012*, dear lower classes of the new order, *la guerre*, the war, *est terminée*, over."

For a moment I worry about the bomb planted under my armchair, and then I remember that, yes, I am the bomb, I am the armchair. There is nothing for me to be afraid of anymore. The war is over.

I whistle a lighthearted melody. My instrument panel indicates that the serotonergic doses have been calibrated, and my enemies' minds will be completely subjugated in a matter of minutes.

I arm the cannons as I fly over the downtown area. On the far side of the mountain, with the McTavish pumping station receding behind me, I randomly shoot people down using gamma rays, and I feel nothing, not even nostalgic about no longer being human. On the contrary, it's good that the future has finally come. Because through everything I've done, from the day I wrote my first sentence until yesterday, the day of my substitution, nothing has sickened me more than my inability to become another, a raven, a hit man, a suffering mother, a so-called victim of the CIA. But from now on I have a feeling of well-being, I am Ewen Cameron, I'm no longer a prisoner of myself, I can create something else, I can become something else. No need to speak, no need to write, I leave novels to the novelists.

I am flying a space ship.

NEVERMORE

MY NAME IS MARION BLOUIN, and I have decided to contact you because a friend called me the other day to tell me about an article in the newspaper *Le Devoir* in which you were said to be working on a book exploring the links between McGill and the CIA.

I underwent treatment at the Allan Memorial Institute, and I would like to share my story with everyone.

I agree to let you write a fictitious story based on my life. There is already a film on the subject starring Macha Grenon; furthermore, the victims have received compensation from the Canadian government.

I find it hard now to tell you everything, not just emotionally but for technical reasons as well. It is difficult for me to go all the way back to the beginning and to proceed according to the natural sequence of events from the past up to the present. Instead, I automatically remember things in the order my memory was programmed to follow, from the present back toward the past.

My mother was a "control freak," and she applied the method she had learned at the Allan Memorial. She was instructed by Dr. Cameroon himself on how to repattern my past.

The first thing I believe to be true is that I was born in 1952 in Cartierville, in the northern part of Montreal.

The second is that at the age of three, on my neighbour's birthday, her husband and two sons shut me in a room and raped me and beat me on the head so badly that I went blind. I was assaulted a number of times, and repeatedly raped.

If my calculations are correct, I was treated at the Allan between 1956 and 1958. I was depatterned so as to forget the abuse I had suffered at the hands of our neighbour, who was also my father's boss, something I believe I have not mentioned.

The neighbour had the means to pay to have my memory erased.

My father, of course, was in a bind because he was dependent on the neighbour. He had to accept. He started to gamble, he started to drink. One night during a quarrel, he tried to kill my mother with an iron bar. I was in a corner of the room and I could see everything.

When my mother regained consciousness, she took

me to my bedroom and applied Dr. Cameroon's method.

I can still hear her saying, "Go back to the past, my little Molly, the part you find ugly, the part where your father tries to kill me with an iron bar. Erase it from your memory and put a pretty story over it." I remember what I answered: "Mom, I cannot return to before, I am after." It was as though she wanted to make sure I would forget, so she incessantly repeated, "To forgive is to forget, Molly, to forgive is to forget."

The way they tried to depattern me did not work, because I have had flashbacks for a long time. The problem with the technique used at the Allan is that its conception of memory is the wrong way round. If in our memories we look at the past from the point of view of the present, the result tends to be greater confusion.

During my teenage years in Cartierville, I got into the habit of taking refuge in the Notre-Dame-du-Bel-Amour church on avenue Jean-Bourdon, to pray.

This was when I realized something was not right. I went back in time and came to the conclusion that my suspicions were justified.

The day before I started kindergarten, my mother warned me: If I said things that were not nice, for example, that Dad hit us with an iron bar, she would send me to reform school, a prison for children who speak badly of their parents. The proof that I was programmed at the Allan is that I didn't understand my mother's warning.

Why would I say bad things about my family if I felt everything was fine?

I reached a point where I had to get out from under my mother's thumb, so I convinced her to let me go to Europe on a trip organized by a Catholic orphanage near our house. The rapport that developed within our group was quite wonderful. We visited several countries, but in Italy something bizarre happened to me.

On a beach on the Amalfi Coast, I was lying on the golden sand next to René-Luc Desjardins, a nice boy who was already engaged, and a future doctor to boot. I trusted him implicitly and the feeling was mutual. All at once, I had an amnesic episode.

When we returned home, the people in the group got together to look at the slideshow of our photos. I was surprised to see a picture of me in the arms of René-Luc. I must add that we both had that twinkle in our eyes, leaving no doubt that something of a sexual nature had taken place between us.

At the time, however, I had no suspicions. My trust in René-Luc was intact. He was engaged to be married, and he was going to be a doctor. Later, however, I wondered whether or not he had depatterned me to make me forget that he had raped me. Perhaps that is why I felt no distress about what had occurred: I had no idea.

A few years later, my investigation led me to discover that René-Luc Desjardins is a colleague of yours at McGill. Can you guess what field he specializes in? He heads the research chair on amnesia.

I decided to get in touch with him to ask for his help in recovering my memory. It was a stratagem. Meanwhile, I learned that René-Luc had had an altercation with the owner of a vineyard, who has since died, apparently a suicide. According to my friend, the woman who saw your name in *Le Devoir*, the cause of death is much more mysterious. It is thought that René-Luc used him as a guinea pig and attempted to erase from his memory an affair that René-Luc allegedly had with the wine grower's daughter during the trip I had been on. His death seems to have been disguised as a suicide so as not to cause trouble for René-Luc's laboratory.

I wanted to get this off my chest. I therefore wrote a letter to McGill stating that if I was given an appointment with René-Luc, I would be accompanied by someone carrying a weapon to protect me. They never replied.

You know, Mr. Farah, my problems really began when I decided to write a book about my experience. When I spoke to my family about this project, they forbade me from carrying it out, saying, "You must not talk about what happened." Once again, I had no idea what my family was referring to. Thanks to Dr. Cameroon's technique, everything was fine as far as I was concerned.

I had no way of knowing all the things that were kept hidden from me.

I assume that, in tandem with the treatments at the Allan, the rest of the family was given instructions, because everyone was united in keeping mum so that I would go on believing that all was well.

An uncle of mine even told me that he could show me how to forget again. It was then that I began to have suspicions, and it dawned on me: the reason I had started to forget my past was because I had been intentionally misled in order for me to forget the violence. I had been implanted with a false story, a story that I had not lived through, and my story had been replaced by other stories.

I do not know if you have children, Mr. Farah, but I find it unacceptable that parents have helped Dr. Cameroon to subject kids to these treatments. Such people were no doubt promised that their offspring would be unable to report them to the police.

Fortunately, because of my book project, I discovered that previously I had been in the "present toward the past" mode; through repatterning, it was possible to take me back to my early childhood and to erase my real story and overwrite it with another in the "past toward the present" mode.

This technique threw me into confusion, and I would like you to understand how uncomfortable it is to live in two periods at the same time.

To put everything back in order, I turned to other approaches. This may surprise you, but, to realign my body, I took part in an exorcism. I plunged directly into my memories in order to stop missing them. In telling you this, I would not want you to think that I have spent my life drinking or taking drugs. Nor that I was under the sway of the Devil. Still, I did decide to seek help. The exorcism did not conform to the ritual of the Catholic Church. Instead, I followed the energy of the planet Mars in a reiki session that enabled an energy realignment of the twenty-two evolving bodies of my aura. After the exorcism, I was able to put an end to the "present toward the past" programming by creating a space where I could travel from the past toward the present and even the future.

Today, I feel that I know my story, but this was not a simple matter. It was my pharmacist who told me, when I consulted him in the little nook meant to ensure privacy, that what I was going through reminded him of patients who had undergone treatment at the Allan. That is when I realized that I was one of Dr. Cameroon's victims.

Thank you so much for going out of your way to listen to me. My lawyer has informed me that, according to treaties to which Canada is a signatory, it is forbidden to impair a person's identity. My goal is to make known that I was subject to an act of torture according to Articles 16, 17, and 18 of the Istanbul Protocol, and I invite all other victims or any journalists who may want to assist me in my investigation to contact me.

Thank you for making the public aware of the danger involved in reconstructing the past on the pretext that by returning to the past one can change the course of history and rid oneself of regrets.

That is not how it works.

Even if we are given medicines and made to listen to messages inside a football helmet, even if someone tries to repattern us to change our story, I do not believe it is possible to live in a saturated, augmented present, or whatever you wish to call it. Try as one may to make us forget childhood traumas, they are recorded deep inside our heads.

Perhaps violence can be replaced by another story. Perhaps they can destroy medical records or tell us that we are not brave, but we will not remain passive.

No, my dear sir, we too will find a way to introduce resources into the past. We will build bases.

I believe that what I have related to you will give other victims the desire to fight, to become aware of the stories told to us in an attempt to repattern us.

Mr. Farah, if everyone came together to eliminate those who want to eliminate us, we would all be healed.

I know how powerful our enemies are. I know they are already developing new techniques. This story is not over. On the contrary, we must now go back to the beginning and start again, and say no: no to the manipulation of the past, no to the manipulation of the present. Only this will allow us to say that we have not suffered in vain. Meanwhile, we must say no, no, I say. The only thing to do is to say No.

(p. 29) *Now I would never diss my own momma*... From Eminem, "Cleanin' Out My Closet," *The Eminem Show*. Shady Records, Aftermath Entertainment, and Interscope Records, 2002.

(p. 53) *Go into Yourself. Find out the reason that commands you to write.* From Rilke, *Letters to a Young Poet*, Trans. Stephen Mitchell (Vintage Books, 1986). p. 6.

(p. 75) *I will not be cured of my youth*... From de Musset, Alfred, *La Confession d'un enfant du siècle*, (Gallimard, 1973). Passage translated from the French by Lazer Lederhendler.

(p. 76) *The satisfaction of knowing that I cured myself*... From de Musset, Alfred, *The Confession of a Child of the Century*, Trans. David Coward (Penguin Classics, 2013). p. 3.

(p. 151) *Water, in the asylum, leads back*... From, Dreyfus, Hubert L., "Foucault et la psychotherapie," *Revue Internationale de Philosophie* 44 (1990): 209-230. Passage translated from the French by Lazer Lederhendler.

à mon frère," Lyrics: Louis Hébert, Music: Philippe Gagnon, 1974. Lyrics translated from the French by Lazer Lederhendler.

ABOUT THE AUTHOR

Alain Farah was born in Montreal in 1979 to Egyptian-Lebanese parents. In 2004, he published a book of poems, *Quelque chose se détache du port*, which was shortlisted for the Prix Émile-Nelligan. In 2005, he set up temporary residence in France to pursue his Ph.D. studies at the École Normale Supérieure. After returning to Quebec in 2008, he published his first novel, *Matamore no 29*. He is assistant professor at McGill University, where he teaches contemporary French literature.

ABOUT THE TRANSLATOR

Lazer Lederhendler is a translator specializing in contemporary Québécois fiction and nonfiction. His work has earned him many distinctions, including multiple nominations for the Governor General's Literary Award, which he won for the translation of *Nikolski* by Nicolas Dickner. He is also the translator of Gaétan Soucy's novel, *The Immaculate Conception*, which was a finalist for the Scotiabank Giller Prize and the Governor General's Literary Award for French to English translation, and the winner of the Cole Foundation Prize for Translation awarded by the Quebec Writers' Federation. Lazer Lederhendler lives in Montreal.